W9-BST-120

Faking 19

Alyson Noël

Faking 19

 St. Martin's Griffin
New York

This is a work of fiction. All of the characters, organizations, and events portrayed in this novel are either products of the author's imagination or are used fictitiously.

FAKING 19. Copyright © 2005 by Alyson Noël, L.L.C. All rights reserved. Printed in the United States of America. For information, address St. Martin's Press, 175 Fifth Avenue, New York, N.Y. 10010.

www.stmartins.com

Book design by Irene Vallye

The Library of Congress has cataloged the first St. Martin's edition as follows:

Noël, Alyson.
    Faking 19 / Alyson Noël.—1st ed.
        p. cm.
    ISBN 978-0-312-33633-2
      1. Interpersonal relations—Fiction. 2. High schools—Fiction. 3. Friendship—Fiction. 4. Schools—Fiction. 5. Los Angeles (Calif.)—Fiction. I. Title.

  PZ7.N67185 Fak 2005
  [Fic]—dc21

2004051168

ISBN 978-0-312-67682-7 (Second St. Martin's Griffin Edition)

Second St. Martin's Griffin Edition: February 2011

10 9 8 7 6 5 4 3 2 1

For Sandy, who believes in blue hippos

Acknowledgments

The following people deserve major thanks:

My mother, for teaching me to read *Horton Hatches the Egg* at an early age, and thereby starting my lifelong love of books.

Fares Sawaya, my high school AP English teacher, who by reading one of my stories aloud changed everything.

Susanne Dunlap, a talented writer, whose generous referral turned out to be the first link in the chain of events that got me here.

My agent, Adam Chromy, whose wisdom, persistence, and expert advice enabled me to realize a dream.

My editor, Elizabeth Bewley, for being cool, smart, and for totally getting what I wanted to say. (And for coming up with a much better title than the one I had!)

Phyllis Taylor Pianka, for the invaluable critiques and an amazing amount of patience.

Robert McKee, an amazing genius and story guru, who taught me to write the truth.

Justine Tumolo, for reading it way before it was ready.

Kenny Blake, Jolynn Benn, the Campbells, the Velazquezes, the Larkins, the Jarrells, the Shermans, and the Rothsteins for simply being there.

But most of all, thanks to Sandy Sherman, who diligently served as loving husband, supportive best friend, motivational coach, legal adviser, personal gourmet chef, comic relief, tireless proofreader, adamant scene turner, bad mood eraser, tech support, and for never, not once, wavering in his belief that it would be done.

Faking 19

Chapter 1

FIVE CELEBRITIES I'D SLEEP WITH IN A SECOND

1. Richard Branson
2. Tobey Maguire
3. Edward Norton
4. Jake Gyllenhaal (sp?)
5. That guy with the dark hair and sunglasses that I saw at Java Daze that time with M that I know is famous but I just don't know what I've seen him in.

Okay, so maybe my list isn't the same as yours. You're probably going, "What's with all the old guys?" or "Richard who?" or "What about Justin Timberlake?" or maybe just, "*Eww!*" Well, technically, I'm a virgin, so the whole list is sort of hypothetical anyway. My best friend M thinks the Richard Branson thing is really sick. She thinks I'm obsessed and swears I've gotten all Freudian since my dad abandoned me. Personally I think M is taking her psychology class a little too seriously.

My parents divorced when I was twelve. I knew it was over when my dad mumbled something about having to find himself as he walked out the door. I swear he was just like Burt Reynolds in *Boogie Nights*. I wish I could tell you about how much I miss him, but the truth is I just wasn't sorry to see him go. That was five years ago, and now at seventeen and a half I can honestly tell you that the only real difference is that these days we're kind of poor, when before we had stuff. Really, that's it. Sometimes it sucks, but for the most part it's totally worth it. I mean, nobody screams in the middle of the night anymore. There's just nothing worse than living in a house where people scream.

I don't remember much about being a little kid. I guess it was an average California childhood. I mean some days I was in trouble and other days I was riding the Matterhorn at Disneyland. I just wanted to go to school, see my friends, ride my horse, eat dessert, and stay up past my bedtime. Those were my goals. Then when a few years passed, and I got a little older, I would just burrow deep under the covers when the screaming started. My sister swears it was really good once. Really happy, just like the Nickelodeon channel. But I can't remember that part. She's eight years older than me, so I guess all that happiness was before I was born. I've pretty much always assumed that I'm a product of make-up sex.

Having divorced parents isn't so bad; when you grow up in Orange County it just makes you normal. Nearly everyone's parents are split, and those who aren't, are like totally on the verge. People here are stuck in a state of permanent adolescence. Most of my friends' mothers take yoga classes and raid their daughters' closets for cool stuff to wear, and their dads watch us a little too closely when we swim in the pool. It's like a continuous midlife crisis, and the parents are like teenagers with credit cards and no curfew. California is like a high school where no one graduates. I'm not kidding.

Anyway, getting back to my "Branson thing," it's not problematic like M says. I'm not obsessed. I just really like him, admire him, and yeah, I think he's sexy. I mean who's supposed to make the list? *NSYNC? The Backstreet Boys? I'm sorry but I just can't go for that prepackaged, focus group, made-for-teens junk. Those guys are like shrink-wrapped with a Mattel stamp on their ass.

I like to think I've developed a more mature, refined taste, but M just swears I've got a daddy complex.

It all started one day last year when M and I were shopping around in this thrift store in Los Feliz (that's in LA). M was in the fitting room squeezing into a pair of old wrecked Levi's and I was just trying to entertain myself when I noticed this book titled *Losing My Virginity* displayed on this gruesome, green coffee table. Thinking it was some kind of "how-to" guide, I eagerly picked it up and started to read. But halfway into the first paragraph I realized it was just a clever title. It's actually Richard Branson's autobiography.

It's not like I hadn't heard of him before, 'cause I think he was on a *Friends* episode or something, but before I saw the book I guess I never really gave him much thought. Well, M decided not to buy the jeans, but I bought the book and I finished it in like a night or two. I guess you could say I'm like a Branson expert now. You could probably ask me anything you want about Virgin Records or Virgin Airlines and I'd know the answer. I know it seems kind of weird, but I can't help it, he's just *so cool!* I mean, he totally sucked at school (like me), so he dropped out and became an entrepreneur. But even though he's worth like billions of dollars now, he's not just some boring business guy that's all about work. It's like, when he's not busy running the Virgin empire, he spends his free time either flying around the world in a hot-air balloon, or hanging out on *his very own* Virgin Island with all of his rock star friends! And he keeps it all organized by making lists every day (also like me), *and* he's a total hottie! (Well, for an old guy.)

But one more thing about Richard Branson, before I forget, I want to make it clear that I don't love him because he's one of England's wealthiest, most famous, men. I'm really not that shallow. I love him because he has the guts, freedom, and imagination to do whatever the hell he wants and that, to me, is incredibly sexy. I guess because sometimes I feel so trapped.

So I daydream, and I admit, sometimes it's a problem. I have a hard time paying attention to boring stuff like economics and all the other senior-year required courses. I used to think that meant

I had attention deficit disorder. I mean, I was seriously worried about that for like six months. So one day I finally bit the bullet and made an appointment with my guidance counselor at school. After what seemed like extensive testing, trying to stay in the circles with a number-two pencil, she told me that I'm okay, I'm just extremely undisciplined, that's all. She also told me, that it's quite possible that I'll never amount to anything if I don't start doing better in my classes. Never mind that, I was just relieved that I wasn't going home with a prescription for Ritalin.

One of my favorite fantasies is about Richard Branson and me in Paris. Just because I've never been to France doesn't mean I can't imagine it. So sometimes during a really long, boring, AP History lecture, I'll sit staring at the chalkboard so my teacher thinks I'm listening. I'll even nod occasionally and scribble stuff on paper like I'm actually soaking in real knowledge, but what I'm really doing is imagining myself, in the Virgin Megastore café in Paris.

I'm seated at a small table in the back and I'm wearing a devastatingly sexy little black dress, strappy high-heeled sandals and black Gucci sunglasses, which are like completely "de rigueur en Paris." I'm delicately sipping a glass of champagne, nibbling on a salmon burger, and reading Paris Match *when Richard Branson walks in. I look up, our eyes meet . . .*

But the truth is, I'm nowhere near Paris. I'm at school, standing in front of my vomit-green locker and I've got exactly three minutes between now and my lunchtime appointment with my mom and my guidance counselor, Mrs. Gross (I swear that's her name). You see, Mrs. Gross wants us all to meet and discuss my "academic goals," that's how she worded it, and I'm wondering if I should tell her that I really don't have any.

Well, my mom is pretty unhappy about having to take time off work 'cause I screwed up, and I know this because she doesn't even want me to meet her in the parking lot and walk her to the office. This morning when I was leaving for school she just gave me that look, the one that tells me she's "this close" to giving up on me, and said, "I'll see you in the office at noon, Alex." Then she lifted her coffee cup and fixed her gaze on an earlier disappointment of mine, a faded, red circle in the middle of the kitchen table, the result of a spilled bottle of Revlon Cherries in the Snow nail polish.

I slam my locker shut and head for the administrative offices, and when I pass the student parking lot I briefly contemplate making a run for it, even though I know I can't really do that. So I tell myself I'll just go in, sit down, let the adults talk, nod my head a lot because they always read more into that than there really is, and soon it will be over.

I see my mother as I'm entering the building but I just glance at her nervously and follow her inside. I mean, we don't smile and hug or even say hello because it's not like I'm about to receive an award or anything.

When we go into the office I just stand there all nervous as I watch my mom and my counselor exchange names and shake hands. Mrs. Gross says hello and motions to two chairs facing her desk. And as I sit down and look around, I give myself a mental lecture for letting it get to this point.

It's your basic school administrator's office. You know, sickly looking plant in the corner, college degrees in gold shiny frames on the wall, and an obsessive-compulsive, fake walnut desk that holds a picture of what looks to be a very happy, if oddly posed family.

Mrs. Gross walks over to a filing cabinet and I watch her fingers deftly crawl over several manila folders until she comes to a big, overstuffed one that she lifts with both hands and places solidly in the middle of her desk. It has my name on it and it lies between us, heavy and foreboding. And I can't stop staring at it while I wonder what I had possibly done up until now that could fill up a folder like that. I mean, I'd always considered myself and my high school experience as pretty mediocre.

She starts leafing through it, giving us a briefing on my entire academic career, and it feels like the moment right before you die when your whole life flashes in front of you. The beginning is all good.

"Well, as I'm sure you know," she says, mauve finger nails scraping between the layers of papers, "Alex was maintaining an A average, even with a challenging schedule of AP classes and several extracurricular activities such as ninth-grade-class vice president, tenth-grade-class president, homecoming princess, French club member . . ."

Blah, blah, blah. I can barely recognize the overachiever she's going on about.

"But lately," she says, "I've noticed a disturbing trend."

My mother leans in closer but I just sit there crouched in my chair, staring at Mrs. Gross's sensible shoes peeking out from under her desk.

"Alex's grades are dropping at an alarming rate. During her junior year she slipped from A's to C's. Last semester she had C's and D's, and I'm afraid her current midterm results are much, much worse." She flips through a couple of papers and shakes her head. "And I'm not aware of her currently participating in any school-sponsored, extracurricular activities." She removes her glasses and rubs the area on the bridge of her nose where they've branded her pink, then puts them back on and continues. "Because of the drastic drop in her grade-point average, her lack of involvement, and her troubling attendance record, Alex is no longer eligible for any of the scholarships she applied for." She looks from my mom to me to see if we are comprehending the weight of all this. I sink down even lower in my chair, and I can feel my mother's refusal to look at me.

"But she was doing so well! Why wasn't this brought to my attention earlier?" My mother asks, shifting the responsibility to the school when the fact is she hasn't asked to see a report card of mine in way over a year.

Mrs. Gross clears her throat and says, "Well, as report cards are mailed to the home on a quarterly basis, I assumed you were aware of Alex's grades." Then she drums her fingers on a pile of papers, and it's my mother who starts to squirm now.

"I'm afraid that Alex is running the risk of jeopardizing all of her prior accomplishments," Mrs. Gross says as she lines up the corners of the papers that reside in my file. "You must understand that those first two and a half years are not enough. It is imperative that she gets her academic record back on track. A scholarship is out of the question. College will be out of the question as well, if we don't see immediate improvement in her grades." She pauses, then looks right at me and says, "I'm afraid that if your grades continue dropping like this you run the risk of failing your senior year and not graduating with your class."

I can feel them both staring at me now, waiting for a reaction. But I just wrap my arms around my waist, making myself smaller, less visible. And even though I heard what she said, I just continue to stare at the ground. I refuse to react because there's no way that could be true. She's just totally trying to scare me, and I won't let her.

I hear Mrs. Gross take a deep breath and say, "I'm not sure how to say this, and I don't want to overstep here, but Alex's behavior patterns, with the dropping grades, and the lack of interest in school activities, well, these are all indicators of chemical abuse."

"But, I've never done drugs!" I shout, forgetting my vow to just wait it out calmly and quietly. I'm out of my chair and I'm facing Mrs. Gross and I just can't stop myself as I say, "Look, maybe I lack involvement or whatever. Maybe I've let things slide. But I don't do drugs, and I never have! I can't believe you just said that to me!"

I'm standing in front of her, frantic and desperate, but she just sits there, regarding me calmly, and I realize that she doesn't believe me. That she's already made up her mind. How can I explain to this sensible-shoe-wearing, Sears-family-portrait-posing, textbook-loving, middle-aged woman that I don't do drugs because I can't lose control. Because my life is so unsound that if I lose control and end up in the back of an ambulance or a squad car there is no one around to bring me back to a safe place. My family is not financially or emotionally equipped to deal with a crisis like that. The only safe place I have is the one I built myself.

I sink back into my seat, cross my legs, and stare at a dirty spot on the floor in front of me. I start to gather my long brown hair into a nervous braid.

"Mrs. Gross," my mother begins, "I assure you that Alex doesn't have a drug problem." She says that with a real tone in her voice. The same tone my sister and I used to get in trouble for (as in "don't take that tone of voice with me, young lady!"). "Now as far as her grades are concerned, I'll keep a closer eye on that and see that she does better." Then she nods her head and looks at her watch, and taps her foot impatiently against the worn tile floor.

Mrs. Gross looks from my mom to me, then leans back in her chair and drops her shoulders in a way that means defeat. And I wish I didn't see that because it makes me feel even worse.

"Okay, Alex," she says. "I want to see some immediate improvement. And let me remind you, once again, that this is a very crucial time where college is concerned. You have to have a plan for where you want to go."

The only place I want to go is *away*. And so I nod my head, so she'll think that I'm already taking action against my sorry self, and follow my mom outside.

The day seems brighter than I remember but maybe it's because everything in that office seemed so dark. I walk behind my mom, struggling in my platform shoes to keep up with her clicking heels and rapid pace, and I'm hoping that she'll stop, and turn, and say something to me, something positive to show that we're still okay.

But when we're halfway to the parking lot the bell rings, and without turning around she shouts over her shoulder, "Alex, go to your next class. You can't afford to be late. We'll talk later."

So I stop and watch her cut through the tide of students until I can no longer see her.

Chapter 2

On my way to AP English I realize that today is the absolutely last day to hand in the *Anna Karenina* critical essay that was assigned exactly eighteen days ago. And suffice it to say that even though Anna, Vronsky, and the oncoming train all made for a pretty good read, I didn't feel like writing about it. So I didn't. I guess that's just the sort of thing that landed me in my counselor's office.

And even though Mrs. Gross says I blew my chances at a scholarship, I know there's just no way this school can flunk me. I mean, so what if I've picked up a bad habit of cutting certain classes. They've got an entire folder full of all the good stuff I've done, and they just can't go failing people for a few C's, some random D's, and a perceived lack of involvement.

I'm gonna go to my English class, make up some excuse for not having my *Anna K* paper, then just sit there and get through it. Just like I did in Mrs. Gross's office (except for that one unfortunate outburst). Then tonight I'll go home and write that stupid paper. And when I'm done with that I'll call my dad and ask him to pay for college. After all, he paid my sister's tuition, and it's the least he can do for me since he never pays child support.

I'm three steps from the door when M runs up next to me and says, "Cool outfit, Alex."

I'm wearing faded, old 501 Levi's that I've decorated with paint and rhinestones and they look just like the ones they sell in trendy boutiques for two hundred dollars. I've paired them with these three-inch platform sandals I can barely walk in, a white, little-boys' tank top, and a vintage, pink cashmere cardigan with a capital A embroidered on it. M and I are totally into clothes. It's a hobby we both take very seriously.

"Did you write your paper?" She's peering at me intently but I don't answer. I don't even look at her. I won't incriminate myself. "Oh my god, you didn't!" She grabs my arm. "Jeez, Alex! What are you gonna do?"

Sometimes I cannot believe that M is my very best friend. I mean, a little support would be nice. I smile at her brightly, and push into class in front of her, but all the while I can feel her eyes watching the back of my head, judging me.

As I walk into class, I avoid eye contact, and sit at my strategically chosen desk. M and I don't sit next to each other. She likes to sit front-row center so she can raise her hand a lot and give correct answers. I prefer to be somewhere in the nether regions of the room, but not too far back. It's not like I want to broadcast my intent to go unnoticed.

Everyone around me is nervously shuffling papers and making last-minute requests for the stapler. And when I look around I realize that none of them will ever be made to suffer the humiliation of a parent/counselor conference because they're the kind of people who do all of their homework, and get good grades, and care deeply about Tolstoy's use of symbolism.

I sit in my wobbly chair, hunch over my desk, and stare at the graffiti etched on it. Someone has carved "YOU SUCK" and I'm wondering if I should take it personally. I don't mean to sound paranoid, but I don't remember it being there yesterday.

I rub my index finger over it again and again, as though that will somehow erase it and make it less true, and when I look up, Christine "the Collector" is standing right next to my desk. So I just watch her stand there, arms heavy with papers, acting like this little extracurricular activity of hers is gonna go on her résumé or something. She taps her creepy, pale pink, acrylic nail against the stack of papers and says, "We're one paper short." She just stands there waiting. "Yup, we're one paper short." She doesn't even blink.

I glance at the headband she's been wearing since she was the hall monitor in fourth grade, and then I look right into her beady, preppy, little eyes, but she's impossible to intimidate, and the only way to get her to leave is to give her something to collect. So I reach into my fake Prada backpack that my sister bought for me in New York and retrieve the short story I worked on all night. It's about a girl who goes to Paris and meets up with an older, English businessman. It's titled "Holly Would." When I hand it over she snatches it, scrutinizes my hand-scrawled mess, and smirks. I'm telling you, she's a total bitch.

I sit there frozen, just waiting for Mr. Sommers to sort through the papers looking for mine, but instead he leaves them in a haphazard pile on the upper-right-hand corner of his desk, puts on a Mozart CD, and begins a discussion about existentialism. M eagerly raises her hand and I relax and sit up a little bit straighter, knowing I'm off the hook today. But tonight he will go home, put on his slippers and start grading papers. By tomorrow he'll know.

"What was that I saw you hand in?" M gives me a suspicious look. "Don't tell me you actually turned in one of your Richard Branson fantasy stories instead of the Tolstoy paper!"

"Okay, I won't tell you." We're walking toward the student parking lot.

"How long do you think you can get away with this?" She looks at me, her face full of concern, mouth twisted with disapproval.

I lean against her car, give her a bored look and say, "At least until tomorrow."

"You're out of control." She shakes her head and opens the car door. "You working tonight?"

I think about how I promised myself I would go home and write my paper and call my dad, and start planning for my future, but for some reason I just shake my head and smile for the first time in two hours.

"Good, let's go into the city."

We get in the little, red BMW Z3 convertible that her parents gave her on her sixteenth birthday. Tan leather interior, marbled wood dash, shiny spoke wheels: I covet this car, but I don't resent her for it. We put the top down, crank the stereo, and put on our faux Gucci sunglasses (okay, M's are real), and head for LA.

Chapter 3

M and I have been friends since I moved to Orange County two weeks before my eighth birthday, and I have to tell you that even at that young age I suffered from culture shock. I had come from a nice, middle-class neighborhood where all the kids played together during the summer and anyone's mom would give you change for the ice-cream truck. Our new neighborhood was totally different. It was all about big houses, big yards, and big gates. There were no block parties, no neighborhood games of kick the can, and definitely no one hawking Popsicles from a musical truck.

On the first day of school I stood in front of the class, nervously chewing on a strand of hair, as my teacher introduced me as the new kid. Everyone just sort of looked me over and ignored me. But M gave me a big smile and invited me to sit with her during lunch, and from that moment on we've been best friends.

I know that on the surface we seem really different. I mean, M's family is rich, mine used to be. M is popular, I'm totally B list. M is a perfect, California blonde, in that, long-haired, blue-eyed, lightly tanned, Kate Bosworth kind of way. I'm dark haired, dark eyed, and kind of quirky, in an Alyssa Milano way. M writes all of her essays, I read the books but rarely complete the assignments.

M just has this amazing ability to totally compartmentalize her life. I mean, on the weekends she can be pretty wild, but during the week it's all about homework and student body activities. I'm not as wild as people think, but I just can't seem to care about school.

But we definitely have things in common too, like we're both totally into clothes, we like the same music, and we're both "gifted." I mean, we scored the exact same numbers on our IQ tests. We just have all this history together and it's a pretty great feeling when someone knows you that well and they still want to hang out with you.

So we end up at our favorite sandwich shack in Venice Beach. There's this really cute guy who works there that I used to have a mad crush on. But he's not into me, because he has a mad crush on M. But she's not into him because she would never date a guy that works in a food stand. She just totally plays him for the freebies. I mean, it's not like she can't afford to buy her own veggie rolls, she just really loves the game.

So she walks up, leans on the counter and goes, "Hey."

That's all she says and he's grinning like a lottery winner. "What's up?" he asks, all excited. His eyes flicker to me briefly then rest on M.

"Well, I'm kind of in the mood for a beer." She lowers her sunglasses and leans on the counter. I think I saw her flutter her eyelashes.

He looks around nervously and says, "Okay, but you've gotta show me some ID or my boss will kill me."

"But you know me, I'm here all the time," she gives him her best smile, the one she saves for school portraits and cheerleading tryouts.

The poor guy just shrugs and I admire him for maintaining some integrity in her presence.

"Oh, all right," she says, making a big show of flipping through the stacks of pictures and little pieces of paper in her wallet. "Damn!" she shakes her head. "You know what? I lent it to Ashley Olsen and that bitch never returned it."

He totally cracks up and puts two veggie rolls and two bottles of water in a bag and hands it to M, free of charge. I mean, the truth is we do have fake IDs, and pretty good ones too, but who wants a beer at three-thirty in the afternoon?

As we're walking away I turn around and I see him looking at her with the most wistful expression. And it makes me really sad. So I promise myself that next time I won't look back.

We find a spot on the sand where we can sit and eat and watch all the stoners and freaky people. That's why we come here. I mean, the shops along the boardwalk are kind of cheesy and the beach itself isn't so great, but the humanity parade is always entertaining.

The boardwalk's pretty crowded today with people strolling, blading, mostly just trying to stay vertical. M takes a sip of her water and goes, "Hey, check out that old guy with the lizard."

I follow the direction of her finger and see some guy walking around in a tie-dyed Grateful Dead T-shirt with this huge iguana perched on his shoulder. He's so weather beaten it's hard to tell how old he is. "You mean the whacked-out dead head? I think I saw him here last week." I squint into the sun.

"Yeah, him. Hey, Jerry's dead!" she yells at him; that really cracks her up. "Man, I love LA," she sighs. "You just don't get this kind of scene back in Orange County."

I nod in agreement. We come from a pretty sterile suburban neighborhood, nothing but minivans and jog-bra moms, a library named after a disgraced ex president, three hundred churches, and not one decent place to get a drink. Our trips to LA have become legend at school. Everyone always wants to come with us but we're very select about who we invite; we usually just hang with each other. My mom probably wouldn't like it if she knew I was coming up here all the time, so I usually tell her that I'm going to the mall or something. I mean, it's not like it's a total lie because we usually do go in shops when we're here.

I watch the iguana man weave down the boardwalk wondering where he's going. He looks so alone that I hope he didn't hear M making fun of him. Then I tear my sandwich into little strips and throw them to a depraved-looking seagull. He spits out the veggies but swallows the bread, another carbo addict. I close my eyes and lie back on the sand; it feels warm and grainy against my skin.

I'm on the French Riviera. I emerge from my lavish cabana wearing a tiny black-sequined, string bikini and a very large-brimmed straw hat. This is a fantasy, so of course I give myself amazing cleavage and a rock-hard ass. Next to my lounge chair waits a turquoise drink with lots of plastic monkeys, paper umbrellas, and a big wedge of watermelon hanging on to the rim. I lie on my belly and take a sip. Suddenly, I feel a warm hand creeping along my spine; I lift my Versace glasses and turn—it's Richard Branson . . .

"So what do you say Alex?" M asks, interrupting my daydream.

"What?"

"You wanna go shopping on Melrose?"

I sit up and shake the sand out of my hair. "Yeah, let's go."

Chapter 4

I f you've never been to LA then let me tell you that it's not a big city like you probably think. It's more like a bunch of suburbs connected by freeways and boulevards. Different areas mean different things, like, Beverly Hills is rich but not as obnoxious as the TV show, and Melrose is way cooler than Heather Locklear.

M squeezes into the world's smallest parking space and we get out of the car and start walking down the street. Hanging out here is the best; sometimes we see famous people. But we don't get crazy about it, we act bored like we're used to it. Just two weeks ago we saw Steven Tyler, you know, that old guy that sings for Aerosmith? Liv Tyler's dad? I mean, you can't miss him, he's all big hair and tattoos, major flamboyance. But when we walked past him we just said "Hey" and kept walking.

"Oh, I love this store!" M says as she walks into some upscale boutique.

I take a deep breath and follow behind wondering if she's gonna have one of her scenes. Every now and then when we go shopping together she'll glide through the store touching all the merchandise and making comments about how she could buy anything she wants, because Daddy's platinum card knows no limits. I guess sometimes she likes to remind me of the economic gulf that divides our families, but I try not to let it get to me. Just because M's parents are like some sort of endangered species still on their first marriage doesn't mean they're happy. I know way too much about her family to be upset by stuff like that.

So I go off on my own and I just sort of meander through the store. There is some seriously cool stuff in here but nothing I can afford. It's weird, because when I'm with M the salespeople are all over us, but just wandering on my own they totally ignore me.

I spot these really cool jeans, they look old and faded and used, and it's amazing how much it costs to buy jeans that someone else has trashed. I take them over to the mirror and hold them against my own, and I run my hand through my hair even though it looks okay. I have pretty decent hair, I mean it's long and dark and wavy, kind of like Alanis Morissette's before she cut it, but my nose is perpetually shiny. I discreetly rub the back of my hand over my nose and adjust the position of the pants.

"Brilliant!"

I look up and there's this really cute guy smiling at me. He's got that kind of messy, brown, Hugh Grant hair, cool clothes, and he's carrying a big shopping bag with the name of this store on it. And I think I heard an accent.

"You like them?" I ask.

"You should get them," he says, nodding.

"So I guess you're not from here," I say, "Are you British?" I clutch the jeans tightly against me. He's so cute it's making me nervous.

"English," he says.

"Do you know Richard Branson?" I blurt out before I can stop myself. God, why did I do that?

"I met him at a party once. Why? Do you know Richard Branson?" He looks at me and smiles.

"Me? No. But I'd like to." I can feel the heat rising to my face. "What's he like? Is he nice?" I ask, noticing how his blue eyes crease up a little bit in the corners when he smiles and wondering how old he is. Definitely not as old as Richard Branson, probably more like twenty.

"Wait a minute." He laughs. "I don't even know your name and I'm already competing with another guy?"

"Oh, I'm Alexandra, but I go by Alex." I smile nervously.

"Alexandra the Great," says M as she walks over eyeing the Brit with interest.

"And your name is?"

"M. Just M."

"Well, I'm Connor, Connor Firth."

He said "Firth" in a way that sounds like "First" and I'm wondering if I'm supposed to know him or something since he gave his first and last name, like maybe he's famous. But it's not familiar so I assume that's just how people in England introduce themselves. You know, like all proper and everything.

We shake hands all around, mine are always so sweaty, but he doesn't seem to notice. "Well, what are you guys doing?" he asks.

M holds up a stack of clothes she's been carrying and goes, "Uh, shopping?"

It sounds kind of rude and I cringe when she says it, but Connor just laughs and goes, "Well, there's an opening at a gallery down the street. I'm headed there now. Would you care to join me?"

I watch M drop the stack of clothes on the nearest rack and go, "Okay." And the way she just said that and the way she's looking at him, gives me this awful feeling that she's really gonna go for him and then I won't stand a chance. I mean, M is beautiful and rich and funny and smart. She's a hard act to follow. And even though I found him first, it definitely won't matter to her. She's used to getting what she wants.

Chapter 5

S o we're walking down the street toward this gallery, with Connor in the middle and M and I on either side, and M is walking all lopsided, like she keeps losing her balance and has to bump into him or grab on to him, but I can totally tell she's doing it on purpose. And it makes me wonder if she really does like him, or if she figured out that I might really like him, and so then she decided to like him just because of that.

When we get to the gallery it's filled with all these trendy people sipping apple martinis and checking out all the other trendy people. The Moby CD they're playing is practically shaking the art off the walls and as I look around I'm pretty sure M and I are the youngest ones here. I mean, everyone else looks like they're pretty sophisticated, you know, like they're in their late twenties or something.

M really gets into this scene. She doesn't know anything about art but then again neither does anyone else. As long as you hold a cocktail, keep circulating, and make really vague comments, no one can tell.

So she's standing really close to Connor now, like she's his date and I'm just some dorky tag-along, and then she squeezes his arm (again) and goes, "Connor, do you think you could get us some wine or something?"

He looks at both of us and says, "Sure, any preference?"

And M (still touching his arm!), smiles and says, "Oh, chardonnay please."

Connor looks at me and goes, "Alex?"

And I go, "Um, red?" like it's a question not an answer. What a retard.

We watch him walk away and then M looks right at me and goes, "Wow, what a hottie. Way to go, Alex."

"What?" I squint at her. I mean, is she kidding? She's been acting like Columbus crawling all over a newly discovered continent and now she's giving me the finder's credit? "Are you kidding?" I ask her.

"What?" she says, and looks at me innocently.

But I just shake my head and don't say anything because I'm not sure what's going on anymore, or what I'm even doing here in the first place. I should be home writing a paper, not hanging in LA, in a scene that I clearly have no part in.

When Connor comes back he's juggling these three glasses of wine and M grabs the white one and goes, "Don't wait up!" then disappears into the crowd, just like that.

I look at Connor and shrug and I hope that he's going to be a little better at the small talk than I am.

We're wandering around the gallery, looking at these big huge oil paintings of what appear to be floating body parts on a sky blue background. And I'm wondering if he understands it any better than I do. Then he turns and looks at me and asks, "What do you make of all this?"

And I go, "Well, um, I think it's really LA."

"What do you mean?" He looks at me intently.

"Well, you know, it's about body parts, and LA is about body parts, for the most part." Oh god, do I sound stupid or what? "I mean, I think it's lonely, really. Like there's an arm over there on that canvas and a knee over on that one and they are all alone because someone has deemed them too imperfect to join the other body parts." I can barely breath.

And then he looks at me, smiles and says, "Thanks for explaining that, I'm always a little confused by modern art."

And I feel totally relieved since I was just talking off the top of my head and I'm not really sure what any of it means either.

So we're just standing there looking at the paintings and I'm desperately trying to think of something to say to fill the growing silence, when I hear someone yell, "Connor! Hey!" And over walks this kind of short, kind of strange-looking guy. And I don't mean strange looking in a genetic way, I mean like he's dressing that way on purpose. You know like black-frame geek glasses, vintage metal band T-shirt, jeans dyed to look dirty, silver Puma tennis shoes, and a black, nylon, man-purse slung over his right shoulder that he probably thinks is a "messenger bag," but it's not. Oh yeah, and his curly, dark brown hair is all brushed and frizzed like Jack Osbourne's.

So Connor goes, "James, hey!" And they both shake hands and then James smiles at me expectantly and I have this momentary fear that Connor might have forgotten my name. Because you know how easy it is to do that when you've just met someone and you're all nervous and you've only heard the name once anyway, but then he goes, "Oh, Alex. James. James. Alex." And I'm totally relieved.

We say hello and I'm expecting to shake hands or something but James leans toward me with his eyes closed and his lips all puckered up. And right when I'm thinking there's no way I'm letting this guy kiss me he makes this loud smacking noise somewhere in the vicinity of my cheek, and I just stand there frozen, wondering if I'm supposed to reciprocate, in this pseudo-European greeting even though we're both American. But then he starts talking about business and stuff so I just try to look involved even though I have no idea what any of it means.

Finally James looks at me and smiles then says to Connor, "Well, I don't want to keep you from your date. Let's do Ivy next week."

And Connor says, "Definitely."

I watch James walk away and ask, "What is 'doing Ivy'?"

Connor shakes his head and laughs and says, "It's a restaurant."

Oh. I guess that's one of those places you're just supposed to know, and not knowing makes me feel like a total outsider and a big loser. "Is he a good friend of yours?" I ask, trying to save myself.

"Not really. I don't mean that he's a bad guy, he's just more of an acquaintance I guess. He owns this gallery. Actually I'm looking for another friend of mine, Trevor. He said he'd be here but I don't see him anywhere." Then he looks at me and smiles and says, "But that's okay, 'cause you're here and you happen to be way better looking than Trevor."

I just sort of stand there and I probably blush, but I don't say anything because when someone tells me I'm attractive I never really know what to say. Not that it happens all the time or anything.

So then Connor starts talking about some of the people who are here tonight. Stuff like, that guy over there works for Maverick records, or that girl with the pink hair is a makeup artist. And even though it's interesting I sort of stop paying attention to the actual words because he's looking at me in the sexiest way and it's making me feel really nervous again.

I start thinking about my virginity. I mean, it's not like I'm very religious, or moral, or even scared (well maybe a little scared). I guess I just never had an opportunity that I could take seriously. Last summer I had this boyfriend for like, a month. I met him on a weekend sail to Catalina with M and her parents. At first I thought he was exotic, you know, from somewhere else, but it turned out he lived in the town next to ours and was still in high school too. So we used to make out and stuff, and at first I was really into him, but it wasn't long before I noticed what a major knuckle dragger he was. You know, like a total caveman. M used to call him Thor. He was really jealous and used to get mad when other guys talked to me. So I had to let him go. I won't have any guy telling me who I can talk to. After that I just figured I would hold out until someone glamorous comes along. I just hope I don't get hit by a car or something first. It would be just my luck to die a virgin.

So I look at Connor and realize I have no idea what he's been saying. I swear my glass of red wine is still half full but my stomach is feeling all queasy and I'm getting kind of dizzy. There's just no way I'm gonna let myself vomit in front of him, so I thrust my glass into his free hand and tell him I've got to get some fresh air.

I push my way through a crowd of people and when I get outside I'm surprised at how cold the night is, but I take off my cardigan anyway and let the cool air just wrap around my shoulders. I look down at the ground and breathe deep and slow just like they taught in the yoga class I took that one time, and I try to convince my mind to convince my body to not puke. To not totally humiliate me in a public place, in front of a totally cute, sexy guy from England, who met Richard Branson at a party once.

When I start to feel better I lift my head and look at the night, and even though I search I cannot locate one star in this polluted LA sky. So I close my eyes and roll my neck and sort of sag against the glass brick wall. Suddenly Connor is there and he's kissing me. At least I think it's Connor. I mean, my eyes are closed so I can't be too sure. It's the most amazing kiss. I just let it linger as long as possible. After awhile I open my eyes and Connor's smiling at me. He brushes his fingers lightly across my cheek and asks me if I'm feeling better now and all I can do is nod, because I'm totally breathless. Then he grabs my hand, entwining his fingers around mine and walks me back into the gallery. That's it. No struggle, no date rape. Sometimes guys surprise me.

I look around the room for M and I see her in the corner talking to some guy in plaid pants. He's completely focused on her and I'm wondering what it is that she's saying. But I guess it doesn't really matter, because there's just something about M that keeps people standing there.

Connor squeezes my hand and says, "I've got to take off soon 'cause I've got an early meeting tomorrow, but I'd really like to see you again. Can I call you?"

So I say "Okay" and act really nonchalant as I'm writing my number down on the back of his card, but inside my chest my heart is hammering and my hand is a little shaky and I really hope he doesn't notice.

He kisses me on the cheek then walks out the door, but I don't turn around to look after him because I don't want to know if he's looking after me, or if he's already moved on to the next big thing. I mean, this night has been practically perfect and I don't want to wreck it by seeing something that might upset me.

On the drive home I ask M about the guy in the plaid pants that I saw her talking to. She just laughs and says that she can't remember his name but that he's British too.

"Do you think he knows Connor?" I ask. I like saying his name.

"I have no idea." She yawns and cranks her new Strokes CD and starts singing at the top of her lungs.

When she turns onto my street, I start to panic because I didn't do what I promised myself I would, and now it's too late to write twelve pages about Tolstoy's technique. And you can bet there will be hell to pay, if not tomorrow then someday soon, because if there's anything I got out of that meeting today, it's that they're watching me now, and I won't be getting away with much.

M drops me off at the bottom of my driveway and asks, "What are you gonna wear tomorrow?".

I open the car door and reach for my backpack that got wedged into the tiny space in the back. "I don't know," I say. "But definitely not denim, I did denim today."

She nods her head and pulls away with a loud screech and I can hear her car all the way to the end of the block.

As I walk up the slope of concrete that leads to my house, I look at the moon and try to determine if it's a man or a woman or something else all together. And I remember how when I was a little kid my mom used to hold my hand and point at the sky and show me how all the dents and craters and shadows could create the illusion of a changing face. I thought there was magic in the moon and we could stand there for hours. But that was back when I believed in things like that, and she believed in me.

I go into my room, throw my purse onto a furry leopard chair, and pick up my phone to check my messages, but I'm greeted with a steady hum so I know no one called. I guess I just couldn't help hoping that Connor had phoned to say how much he enjoyed meeting me, even though I know how totally improbable that is.

But there's a call I have to make, and I glance at the glowing numbers on the alarm clock next to my bed and wonder if 10:52 is too late. It might be, but I call anyway. While I listen to it ring I rehearse what I'm going to say. But on the fourth ring it goes straight into voice mail so I just go, "Hi Dad, it's me. Um, Alex. Can you give me a call? It's important. Thanks." And then I hang up feeling kind of relieved that I didn't actually have to ask him because he's my only hope now and I'm not really sure what he'll say.

I wash my face, brush my teeth, and put on this soft, pink, vintage slip that I like to sleep in. I climb into bed and the sheets feel cool and the blanket is warm, and I know that when I wake up I'm going to have to face Mr. Sommers about the paper I didn't write, but I don't want to think about that now. So I try to think about dining with Richard Branson at the restaurant at the top of the Eiffel Tower, but Connor's head keeps appearing on Branson's body.

Chapter 6

The next morning my mom peeks her head in my room to make sure that I'm up and thinking about getting ready for school. I assure her I'm wide-awake, then roll over for another ten minutes.

She's back. "Alex, I'm not kidding. I'm leaving for work now and you better get up or you'll be late for school."

"Is that the worst that will happen?" I ask her.

"Alex, now!"

"I'm up."

I wait until she leaves my room then I crawl out of bed and go into my bathroom and turn the shower on high and hot. I sit on the closed lid of the toilet seat and watch the room get all steamy. The dream I had last night is still lingering but it wasn't about Richard Branson or even Connor. It's that same old recurrent nightmare about when my horse died.

I was in the seventh grade and it was a terrible time. It was not long after my dad left, and next to M, my horse, Lucky, was like my best friend. One day when I went to feed her I found her in her stall just lying there. I got scared and called the vet. He gave her shots and vitamins, he did everything he could, but after three days he said he just couldn't help her and he'd have to put her to sleep.

I really hate that term, "put to sleep." Sleep is when you get to wake up. And it didn't help knowing that my dad had just bank-rolled some gorgeous thoroughbred at some cushy stable for his lat-est girlfriend. I think my horse died of poverty, exposure, and depression, just another casualty of the divorce. I tried to love her enough to keep her alive, I really did. But she died anyway. I guess it's just as well since we could barely afford to feed her. Horses re-ally eat a lot.

I climb into the shower and lather up. I'm big into grooming. In an average shower I use shampoo, conditioner (deep conditioner in the summer), lavender-scented shaving gel, facial cleanser, facial scrub, and body cleansing gel, followed by body scrub. While my skin is still damp I spray on body oil, which I let soak in for about sixty seconds, then I lightly pat my skin dry and apply body lotion, deodorant, astringent, lip balm, leave-in conditioner, and a tiny bit of some perfume sample. This month it's Gucci Rush be-cause I like the name. I'm a total product whore.

With a towel turban around my head and a robe wrapped tightly around me, I stand in front of my closet looking for something to wear. I mean, I've spent the last three and a half years building a fashion reputation and now everyone expects me to show up in something cool and unusual and sometimes it's a real burden.

And I'm thinking maybe that was the wrong approach, draw-ing that kind of attention to myself. Maybe I should tone it down a little, you know, work a little harder at blending in. So I slip into the safety of some faded, denim overalls, a lacy camisole, an antique-beaded cardigan, and my split toe Nikes. I quickly brush on a little mascara to accentuate my brown eyes and grab two rub-ber bands and braid my wet hair during the red lights on my way to school.

I see M in French class. And I don't mean to be rude but she's got a pretty major zit on her chin, and I can't stop staring at it. You know how trying not to look at something just makes you obsessed with it? Well, that's what it's like with M's chin. At least she didn't try to cover it with makeup like some girls, 'cause that never really fools anyone. But it's still kind of funny to see M looking less than perfect.

She sees me staring so I go, "Rough night M?"

"Very funny," she rolls her eyes. "I thought you said absolutely no denim today."

"I almost wore my pajamas," I tell her.

"I know what you mean. I'm feeling a little sleep deprived, but it was totally worth it, don't you think?"

"Totally." I look around the room to see if anyone's listening. I have to admit we usually talk loud enough so everyone can hear, but then we get annoyed when we catch them.

M leans in and says, "That guy in the plaid pants called last night. He must have dialed right after we left 'cause there was a message from him when I got home."

"No way." I look at her in amazement. Even though I'm used to M always stealing the show, I can't help feeling a little jealous. "Did he leave his name?"

"No. He just started talking so I still don't know it. Oh, and I got accepted into Princeton! The letter came yesterday when we were in LA. The maid put it in my room."

I'm staring at M with my mouth wide open when Mademoiselle walks in. "Bonjour!" she says.

"Bonjour Mademoiselle!" I hear my classmates answer, but I can't concentrate now because all I can think about is how my life totally sucks compared to M's. She's got a new boyfriend, and she's going Ivy. I've got an empty voice mailbox, and I may not get out of high school. I mean, I'm happy for her, really I am, but there's a part of me that feels like vomiting.

I manage to slide through the rest of the day. Partly because we have a sub in Economics (I hate that class), so I don't even pretend like I'm paying attention, and partly because Mr. Sommers makes absolutely no mention of the paper I didn't write. It's like he still doesn't know or something, and I'm hoping that will buy me an extra day or two since that's all I really need because I'm totally gonna do it tonight, after work. I promise.

After school I go to work for four hours. I've been working in this department store for like a year and a half. I entered this contest where they picked one student from each local high school and the winners got to be in what is called Teen Board. It involved in-store modeling, fashion shows, charity events, and a job for anyone who was interested. I was really nervous at the interview and totally didn't expect to be chosen. I mean, all of the usual suspects showed up, you know, the cheerleaders and supermodel wannabes, everyone clutching their portfolios. I didn't have a portfolio, just the application and some majorly sweaty palms.

I was only there because I needed a job. Those child-support checks were getting few and far between, and quite frankly, I was sick of begging for them. Believe me, I never took the modeling part seriously. I'm not like all the other girls in my school carrying around composite shots and taking voice lessons. That's the funny thing about California, life somehow becomes one long audition. Anyway, for whatever reason, they picked me and I've been working here ever since. The modeling part was fun, I'll admit, but when it was over I didn't really miss it. This isn't the most exciting job, but it's decent. I mean I get to work with nice people and I get a good discount on clothes.

Well, a couple of months ago the managers here transferred me from the Junior Department over to Women's. They told me they thought I was very mature and could handle a more professional group. That really cracked me up. I mean, I never really think of myself as being mature. But I have to admit I like being over here. The women I work with are really nice. They worry about me and give me advice. I usually don't like it when people act like that with me, like I need help or something, but it is kind

of nice when these ladies try to make it easier. The other difference about working over here is how these customers, who are
like my mom's age, talk so freely about their cheating husbands
and plastic surgeries. I just give them a sympathetic look, and
vow to never grow old.

The store is dead on Friday nights. I guess most people have
better things to do than shop. So after I refold all the cashmere
sweaters and try on a few leather jackets, I pretty much spend
the rest of the time making a list of the five things Richard Branson and I would be doing during a Virgin transatlantic flight.
Canoodling is at the top. I don't really know what it means but
they're always accusing Julia Roberts of it in *People* magazine so I
figure it must be good.

My phone rings and it's my friend Blake calling from the
Men's Suits Department where he works. Blake was on the Teen
Board the year before me, he's the one that got me into this. He's
also gay, but he's way open about it so he's definitely not going to
mind my mentioning it.

"Alex, what are you doing?" he asks.

"Oh, just leaning on the cash register, staring into space, making lists. Hey, what does *canoodling* mean?"

"It's sexual."

"Yeah, but what exactly?"

"Cuddling?"

"Oh, is that all? Are you sure?" I ask.

"No, I let my subscription to *Teen People* expire. Hey, what are
you doing later? Do you want to get a coffee or something?"

"Well, I told M I'd meet her at the baseball game tonight." I
lean against the cash register and look in the mirror.

I can practically hear Blake rolling his eyes when he says, "You
did not just say that. A baseball game?"

"Yeah, it's a night game, but it should be over by the time I get
there. God willing. Wanna go?" I ask.

"Honey I am never going back to that place."

Blake graduated a year ago.

"And I can't believe you'd choose sports over me. C'mon, I'll even pay."

"Really?"

"Yes, really."

"Well in that case . . ."

At about ten minutes to nine I start closing out my register. I count the change as quietly as I can because the management here doesn't like it when you start early. Then I just stand there until exactly nine o'clock and then I bolt upstairs to deposit the money. I see Blake on my way up. We both look at each other and then we start tearing for it, I mean, really running. I'm gaining on him big time until my heel catches on something and I go soaring and crashing. But I'm not hurt. I just lay there laughing on the floor, right next to some home furnishings display. Blake feels bad for me so he comes over to see if I'm okay. I give him my hand so he'll help me up, and then right when we touch I pull him down and I jump up and beat him to the deposit spot.

He walks up behind me, rubbing his elbow, and saying, "I can't believe you'd cheat like that."

And I go, "Yeah, well, I really do have ambition, it's just usually about all the wrong things."

So we end up in this generic coffee place somewhere between work and home. It tries to be hip but it's really not that cool, and I'm not even going to mention the name because there's already one on every corner and they don't need me to advertise for them.

I order a decaf latte, and try not to feel bad about ditching M. But let's face it, I barely go to school during the day, why would I go at night?

"So what's new with Ronette?" I ask as we sit down. She's the manager of the Men's department. Her real name is Rhonda but we secretly call her Ronette, because she has totally retro hair, and, well, she's kind of a bitch.

"Honey, I can't wait to give her my two weeks notice," Blake shakes his head and takes a bite of his almond biscotto.

"When are you leaving for Parsons?" It's a question I've avoided asking.

"Soon. June."

"What?" I practically choke on my latte, that's only three months away.

"I want to spend the summer there. You know, find an apartment. Get settled in, check out the scene."

I sit there staring at him. "Um, not to be selfish or anything, but what am I going to do without you?"

"Come with me." His oversize coffee mug hides most of his face, but his eyes are right on mine.

"If only." I look down at my cup and put my head in my hands. I don't have the talent for design like Blake does. I don't have any talent. It feels like everything is creeping up and closing in. I wish I could just stop time until I was ready for it to happen.

"Have you been accepted anywhere yet?"

I don't answer.

"Are you okay?" he asks, concern in his voice.

"Yeah, yeah." I look up at Blake and give what I hope will come off as a confident smile.

"Alex, you're smart and talented. You can do anything you want," he says.

"Oh, please," I shake my head. "Nobody wants me. Well, that's not entirely true. There's one loser school that kind of wants me, but yesterday I found out that my grades suck so bad that I no longer qualify for a scholarship. And if they don't get better then I won't qualify for admission. And they're even trying to tell me that I might not get out of high school, but there's no way that's true. They're just trying to freak me out. Oh yeah, and I called my dad to ask for help but he won't call me back."

"Why won't he call you?"

I shrug. "I guess he's just really really busy."

"So, why don't you visit him at his office or something?"

"Because if he says no, then what will I do?"

"Why would he say no?"

"Because, for the seventeen and a half years that I've known him, he's said it an awful lot." I stop and take a sip of my coffee. "But he owes me this, he really does."

"Alex—"

I hold up my hand. "Could we please not talk about it?"

"All right." He gives me a concerned look and says, "I just want you to know that you have more options than you think."

Chapter 7

So instead of going home and writing my paper, I stop by M's to see if she's there because I feel kinda bad about not showing up at the baseball game. And as I park on the street and get out of my car, I wonder why the promises I make to other people always become more important than the ones I make to myself.

As I walk toward the front door I hope that her parents aren't home. I guess they're not that bad, but it's always better when they're not around. I mean, M's mom really doesn't do much except think about her weight, it's like she's a professional size two or something. And M's dad makes me call him "Doctor" because he is one. Still, what an ego. I mean, he's a plastic surgeon doctor, not a real doctor. He saves noses, not lives.

So M opens the door and says, "Hey what happened? You weren't at the game."

"I had coffee with Blake," I tell her as I walk inside and head for the living room 'cause that's where we always hang out. When I hear a voice I stop and look at M and whisper, "Are your parents here?"

M shakes her head, "No, it's just Tiffany."

"What? Why?" I stand in the hall. Tiffany is my least favorite of all of M's fellow cheerleaders.

"She had to pick up a sweater I borrowed at the game last week, and now she won't leave. She's wasted too, you've gotta see it," M says as she pushes me into the living room.

"Hey Alex!" Tiffany waves at me from the couch.

"Hey Tiff, what's up." I plop myself onto an overstuffed arm-chair and grab one of the beers sitting on the table.

"Well," she slurs, "I was just telling M that I'm totally considering breaking up with Dylan, even though I totally love him."

M shakes her head and rolls her eyes, and picks up the remote control for the stereo. And I'm left with no choice except to ask, "Why are you breaking up if you still love him?"

"Because I'm so sick of him flirting with other girls." She starts crying then and I look at M totally alarmed, but she has her eyes closed, singing along to some Alicia Keys CD.

"He was totally flirting with Amber tonight, you should have seen him. And I got so mad I just left without him. I even fell off the top of the pyramid, but he didn't care."

"Are you okay?" I ask her. For some reason I'm genuinely concerned.

"My arm kind of hurts, but the point is he didn't even notice! And I love him. I love him so much, and I don't understand why he always flirts with her. She's not that pretty!"

I just look at Tiffany and I want to tell her that life really isn't one long beauty contest. That everyone's just trying to find what makes them feel good, but I don't say anything. I just hand her a tissue, and wish she'd stop talking because she's really starting to depress me.

Then she clutches her stomach and says, "Oh, I don't feel so good." And I watch her run for the bathroom.

M opens her eyes and goes, "Dammit. She better make it in time, 'cause I'm not cleaning that up."

"How much did she drink?" I ask.

"Three of those empty bottles are hers. I've been putting up with this shit for like an hour now and I'm totally over it." M sits up and puts down the remote and looks at me. "Tiffany is such a loser. She's all upset over some retard jock. I swear, high school is so small time. I am so over it." She shakes her head and takes a sip of her beer.

I look up then to see Tiffany standing in the doorway and at first I'm afraid she might have heard us. But she just goes, "M will you take me home? I don't think I should drive."

Tiffany's clutching her stomach and she looks pretty bad, but when I look at M she looks really mad, so before she can say anything I go, "I'll take you home Tiffany. I was just getting ready to leave anyway."

I take one last sip of my beer and grab my purse and guide her out the front door to my old Karmann Ghia that used to belong to my sister. I put her in the passenger seat and buckle her in and she just sits there with her eyes closed. And even though throwing up didn't make her sober, I'm thankful that it made her quieter.

When we get to her house her eyes are still closed and I can't tell if she's passed out or dead of alcohol poisoning. So I tap her softly on the shoulder and say, "Tiffany, wake up. You're home."

And then she opens her eyes and bolts out of my car and runs straight for her mother's prized rose bushes where she vomits orange all over them for like the next five minutes.

I get out of my car and watch her and I'm torn between being totally grossed out, and hoping that her parents don't wake up, see this mess, and hold me responsible.

When she's finished I hand her another tissue and walk her to the door and assure her that she'll feel much better in the morning, which is a total lie because once the hangover sets in, it will be much worse.

As I'm driving home I look at all the sleeping houses, all locked up and tidy until morning. And from the outside everything looks so protected, so safe. But you just never know what kind of lives are being lived in those houses. I mean, you just never really know anyone. Like Tiffany, it was weird watching her break down like that. It's not that I thought she was without feelings, it's just that at school she always acts so perfect and together, like nothing bad ever happens to her. So it was really surprising to see her crying over some guy and heaving in the rose bushes.

And I remember how I used to be like Tiffany. How I used to care about the things that happened at school. How I used to be part of that ruling class of cool kids that spend most of their time making everyone else feel bad about not belonging. I used to take it seriously too. But then my parents started regressing, and messing up at all of the things they were supposed to be guiding me through, and it forced me into a whole new set of problems. I mean, once you start worrying about your mom's mortgage payment, you can't really worry about Sadie Hawkins with the same intensity that you used to.

So when I get home the first thing I do is go into my room and check my messages: nothing. No one called. Not even Connor. But it's only been a day. Usually guys wait longer than that, right? Well, unless you're M. When you're M, they're dialing your number before you even get home.

But my dad didn't call either so that means I'm gonna have to call him again. And I can't believe it's gotten to the point where I'm dependent on the one person I could never depend on.

I dial his number with a shaky hand, and when it goes into voice mail I leave the same stupid message as last night.

Then I put on an old T-shirt with a faded picture of Lisa Simpson, and instead of starting my paper, I lie on my bed and look at this month's *Vogue*. I fall asleep wishing I looked like Gisele Bundchen.

Chapter 8

Saturday afternoon I'm staring at the cover of *Anna Karenina* and a blank piece of paper when M calls. "Alex, did Tiffany barf again on the way home?"

"No, she was fine," I lie. For some reason I don't feel like telling her about the rose bushes.

"Well she missed the toilet, and the poor maid had to clean it up."

"So why didn't you do it if you felt so bad for her?" I put down the book and pick at a hole that's forming on the knee of my sweatpants.

"Yeah, right. Oh my god, I forgot to tell you. Tiffany totally fell off the top of the pyramid last night!" M is cracking up. "You should have seen it! She just went flying off the top and hit the ground!"

"Yeah. She mentioned it. But she seemed fine," I say.

"She seemed fine because she was so drunk she was feeling no pain."

"You mean she was drunk at the game?"

"Big time . . . Amber brought these little water bottles full of vodka for everyone, and they were all like totally guzzling in the parking lot before the game. But I gave mine to Tiffany because

I don't like vodka without juice, and she totally downed that too. Everyone was fine except her. She can't handle drinking. What do you bet she shows up Monday morning in a neck brace or something? I swear she did it on purpose."

"That's ridiculous."

"Not really. I think she was trying to get Dylan's attention, but he didn't even notice."

"Why are you guys doing pyramids at a baseball game anyway?" I ask. Everything cheerleaders do is a mystery to me.

"Because school's almost over, it's our last chance. So anyway, listen, there's a major party tonight in LA and we're invited."

"Really?"

"Yeah, that guy that I met at the gallery, the one in the plaid pants? It's at his house."

"Did you remember his name yet?"

"As far as I'm concerned it's Plaid Pants because I still don't know it."

"You're kidding?"

"No, really. When he called he just said, 'Hey,' and I went, 'Hey,' and I totally missed my chance to say 'Who is this?'"

"Well, how did you know it was him?"

"The accent, he's British. Anyway he's having some big bash and he told me to bring a friend if I want. Are you in?"

"I guess," I walk across my room, peer into the mirror, and hold up the back of my hair, wondering if I should cut it.

"What do you mean? You've got something better to do?"

"Well, I really should write that stupid paper for English," I say.

"Do it tomorrow. C'mon Alex, it's gonna be great."

"Well," I twist my hair back really tight and try to imagine what I'd look like with a pixie cut, "I was kinda hoping that Connor would have called by now."

"He hasn't called yet?"

"No."

"Well forget him. There's gonna be tons of hotties at this party tonight, we'll find you a new one. Are you in?"

"Yeah, I'm in." I drop my hair and watch it fall, stopping just short of my waist.

"Good. Apparently it started at noon, but I'll pick you up at seven, we don't want to look too eager."

When I hang up I'm in a total panic about what I'm gonna wear. M will just grab daddy's plastic on her way to the mall, but I don't have that luxury, so I have to come up with something hip with what I've already got. I'm usually pretty good at this, you know necessity being the mother of invention and all. But today I'm a little short on inspiration. I put on a Hole CD and listen to Courtney scream about wanting the most cake. Yeah, me too. I crank up the volume and head down the hallway to my sister's old room.

Every time I look in her closet I'm amazed at all the clothes and shoes she left behind. I mean, it looks like she was in such a hurry to bail out of here that she didn't bother to pack. I come across a slinky old prom dress of hers that still carries the faint scent of Obsession perfume, and run my fingers over the silky fabric remembering how she always used to spray that on her clothes so my parents wouldn't know she'd been smoking.

I pull off the sweatpants and tank top I've been wearing all day and slip the dress over my head. I'm the same size now that she was then so it fits perfectly. I stand in front of the mirror and gaze at my reflection. I like the shiny cream color and the deep V-neck and spaghetti straps. The only problem is the length, which is nearly to the floor, and since it's not my prom night, that just won't do.

I gather the fabric around my waist, then I go back into my room where I put on these really cool, strappy, high-heeled sandals that I bought at a thrift shop last year and glued tiny silk flowers all over. I know it sounds kind of overdone, but trust me, it works. On top of my dresser is a little tiara barrette I bought in the children's department at the store where I work. I pull the top part of my hair back, like J Lo does, and secure it. It might be a little too fairy princess, but I like it. So then I take everything off and lay it on my bed and get to work on hemming the dress.

I like to sew. I learned how in my fourth grade Girl Scout troop. It's probably the most useful skill they taught me besides making s'mores. I mean, since I love clothes and I don't have much money, I mostly go to thrift stores, buy stuff cheap, then bring it home and tweak it. That way I never look exactly like everyone else because mine is one of a kind. I also find it calming. I like the hum of the machine when I do a really long seam.

I start thinking about Connor even though I promised myself I wouldn't. I just can't figure out why he hasn't called yet. It seemed like we were having such a great time together. But since I didn't get his number it's not like I can call him. Not that I would anyway.

My mom talks about the giant steps that women have taken since she was my age, but I just don't see it. I mean, maybe we can vote and stuff but there's still these really burdensome social rules that just won't change, like sex. It may seem like everybody in your school is doing it, and most of them probably are, but let's face it, girls that experiment get labeled as sluts, while the guys get the stud trophy. And that's why there will be no sweaty high school stuff for me. No getting biblical in the backseat with some icky senior. And as far as calling guys first, I won't do it. I truly believe they still want to go out and hunt and conquer and drag you home by your ponytail. We may live in the suburbs, but we act like a bunch of cave dwellers.

When I'm finished hemming the dress I press the new seam with a warm iron and put it back on. It looks pretty good. I have about twenty minutes left so I apply a little makeup (with an outfit like this you don't want to go overboard), flip my hair a few times, put on some glittery nail polish, and then dance around with my arms in the air until it dries.

When I hear M's car pulling into my driveway I jot off a quick note to my mom telling her that I'm spending the night at M's.

I feel bad about lying, but I don't want her to worry. The truth is, these LA parties usually go on until the next morning.

M sees me and says, "Cool dress!"

I pirouette on my driveway then climb into her car. I turn down the vintage David Bowie CD she's got blasting and say, "Okay, details."

She looks at me and smiles. "This could be it, the most important party so far. The one we've been working toward."

"What?" I have no idea what she's talking about.

"Okay, get this. Plaid Pants is a film student at USC and his parents are like producers or directors or something in the industry, but apparently they are very conveniently tucked away on vacation or location or whatever in Europe. They've got this fully loaded house. You know like pools, a guest house, screening room, the works."

"Who's gonna be there?" I ask, wondering if Connor could possibly show up, but I don't ask it out loud because I don't want to jinx it.

"Probably like tons of rich, young Hollywood types, because of his parents and film school and all. We might even get to see a celebrity or something."

"You mean like Richard Branson?" I ask.

"No. Probably more like that girl who plays Sabrina the Teenage Bitch."

I look at her to see if she's kidding but she's totally serious and I suddenly start to feel really intimidated and sick to my stomach. It's not about some minor TV star, it's just that all that wealth sometimes makes me feel totally inadequate. I remember reading somewhere that no one can make you feel intimidated without your permission. Well, Plaid Pants has got my full consent. I mean, I'm just not so sure I can blend with this crowd. People with that much money always make me feel like an outsider.

M looks at me, and knows what I'm thinking. "Relax," she says, "it's gonna be fun."

And I look at her and wonder again, as I often do, just where her endless supply of confidence comes from. Is it the birthright of the wealthy, of having the security of two parents and a team of lawyers who will always be there to clean up your mess?

Chapter 9

When we finally get to the house, M drives right past all the cars lining the street, swerves around the Mercedes spooning the Porsche in the driveway, and goes right onto the front lawn where she hits the brake and kills the ignition. She double-checks her lip gloss in the rearview mirror, then smiles and says, "We're here!"

There's a rose bush banging against my window and I think there's another one under the car, but this is classic M, she always makes it easy for herself, and she always gets away with it. I look at her and say, "Jeez, why didn't you just drive into the living room and park next to the sofa?"

She pulls the key from the ignition and shrugs. "I'm not about to walk all the way down the block in these boots."

She holds her foot up for inspection and I can't say I blame her. She's wearing her wicked witch boots, the sleek, knee-high, black, pointy-toed ones, with heels so high it must be like walking on stilts.

We walk the three steps to the front door and when we open it we are confronted with a wall of bodies. I mean, there's like, hundreds of people here, and we just stand in the entryway trying to get a handle on the scene, but I don't see any celebrities, just a lot of people who want to be celebrities. There's a group of tall, blond, tan girls wearing bikinis and Ugg boots, they look like quintuplets, and another group wearing low-cut jeans and newsboy caps, total Britney clones.

There's even some guy walking around in a silk robe, but it's not Hugh Hefner. And even though I can kind of make fun of them in my head, the truth is, that everyone here looks like they belong, and I start to feel kind of stupid in my old dress and tiara. I mean, I might have looked okay in Orange County, but here, around all these hip, rich people, I feel like a dork.

I reach up and touch my stupid rhinestone barrette and contemplate yanking it out when, M looks at me and goes, "Don't. Leave it. You look great."

And I stop, and I leave it, because she's right. I have to be comfortable just being me.

"Come on," she says, "let's grab a drink and find the screening room."

We grab some champagne from a passing waiter then follow the scent of popcorn down a long hallway. We enter a dark room with a big screen and plop into some vacant seats. They have the same seats as the good movie theaters, you know, the plushy kind that rocks back and forth, with cup holders. I place my drink in the little hole and lean all the way back and look at the high, vaulted ceilings. It must be so cool to have a room like this. I mean, at my house it's just an old TV with a broken remote and no cable. It's amazing how other people get to live.

There's like, six guys and one girl in here, and they're all watching some really violent movie. M gets up to get popcorn but I'm ready to leave. I hate gratuitous violence. I mean, isn't there enough of the real thing out there? Like in Afghanistan, and Africa, and that school in Colorado, and the house next door?

I follow her and go, "M, are you gonna watch this?"

She whispers, "Yeah, at least until I finish this popcorn, why?"

"Well, I think I'm gonna leave and walk around some more."

"Okay," she says between bites. "Listen, if we lose each other, meet me by the front door at midnight."

I squint my eyes to adjust to the light of the hallway and wander down it, unsure of my destination. I figure I'll just walk around until something interesting happens. At a party like this, it shouldn't take long.

I'm just walking along, looking at the art on the walls, when all of a sudden a door right in front of me opens and I'm face to face with Connor. My heart skips, my stomach drops, and I stop dead in my tracks. I just stand there staring at him like a major dweeb when he looks up and goes, "Alex!"

"Oh. Connor. Hi." I'm trying to pretend that I didn't see him first, but it's not very convincing.

"It's brilliant to find you here." He's hugging me now and he smells so good, and even though I dreamed of this every night since we met, now that it's happening I can't remember any of my lines.

So I'm just standing there staring at him, trying to think of something to say when this really pretty girl who looks just like Ray of Light Madonna comes out of the same room he just vacated and goes, "Connor, there you are!"

When I watch her slither up next to him and put her hand possessively on his shoulder, I start to feel sick and nervous and I don't know what to do, so I just continue to stand there like a big retard and then I smile at her. Only she doesn't smile back.

Then Connor goes, "Sam this is Alex. Alex, Sam." And since nobody got a title like, My Girlfriend Sam, or, The-Best-Thing-That-Ever-Happened-to-Me Alex, it's hard to tell how either of us rates.

I just stand there and say, "Hi." Giving another go at a smile.

But she just presses her lips together in a failed attempt at a pleasant expression and says, "So how do you know Trevor?"

"Um, who's Trevor?" I ask, looking from Sam to Connor and wondering if I should have just faked like I knew him.

"Uh, your host?" she says, and rolls her eyes, and shakes her head, and looks at Connor like, "Who is this loser girl you found in the hall?"

But Connor just smiles and says, "He's the guy I was looking for at the gallery the other night. I think M met him there."

"Oh, I didn't realize that was his name," I say. But I don't mention that up until now we've been calling him Plaid Pants.

"You know I was wondering if you'd be here."

"Really?" I'm trying to not sound too excited by that.

"Yeah." He smiles and his eyes travel over me, coming to rest on my chest. "Where's M?"

"Watching something violent in the screening room," I tell him. Then I look over at Sam but she's busy inspecting her wavy, long blond hair, looking for split ends or something, and not at all trying to hide the fact that she's bored, and mad, and everything else.

"Uh, Connor, excuse me," she says tugging on his sleeve, "Are you coming back in, or what?"

I just stand there and look from her to him but he just shakes his head, and goes, "No, I'm taking Alex on a field trip. I'll catch up with you later." Then he looks down at me and smiles and I feel like I've been thrown into the deep end of the pool.

Connor puts his arm around my shoulders and walks me down the hall, and I look up at him and say, "I have to warn you, M has given me a twelve o'clock curfew."

"Great. That leaves us with . . ." He stops and looks at his wrist but he's not wearing a watch, "Well, lots of time, I hope."

Then he leads me through some French doors out to this beautiful garden. It's one of those wild, untamed, English-style gardens that make you feel like you're in *Wuthering Heights* or something. He points out all the different varieties of flowers, then stops to pick a really beautiful pink peony. When he hands it to me I wonder how he knew that's my favorite.

We walk by the pool but there's some people splashing around in it, so instead we go inside this really cool cabana. The walls are a dark, smudgy, salmon color and it's stuffed with pillows and hammocks and mosquito nets and lanterns and loads of colorful mosaic tiles, and it looks just like a movie set version of Morocco. I sit on this woven mat and lean back against these giant, over-stuffed pillows, and watch Connor light a few candles and look through the fridge for something to drink.

"Is this a guest house?" I ask, rubbing my fingers over a se-quined pillow.

"No, it's just a cabana, the guest house is farther down," he says.

I watch him walk toward me carrying a bottle of champagne and place it on a low tiled table. The way he just answered me so casually makes me wonder if he grew up like this too. I mean, it's hard to be that blasé about homes like this unless you're used to it.

"You don't think they'll mind?" I ask, eyeing the bottle of champagne with the label I can't pronounce even after four years of high school French.

"Mind what?"

"If we drink their champagne?"

"Not only will they not mind, they won't even notice."

I watch Connor expertly pop the cork, refill my glass, and grab a pillow and lie next to me with his head propped on his el-bow. He's looking at me intently and the fact that he's a total babe, along with the fact that we're completely alone is making me in-credibly nervous. Also, the silence is growing thicker and it's mak-ing me feel like I've got to say something interesting right exactly now but I can't think of anything. Then I remember this article I read in *Cosmopolitan* that said you should just let them go on and on about themselves. Not that I'm used to following that kind of advice, but right now, when I'm feeling this shy and nervous, it does come in handy. So I go, "How do you know Trevor?"

"I've known him since we were kids. We were schoolmates in London, until his parent's packed it up and moved out here.

"When was that?" I ask.

"I don't know, fifteen? Sixteen?"

He looks at me and smiles and I nod my head and take a sip

of champagne as I desperately grasp for something to say next. "So, tell me about your record company? How'd you get started?" I ask. Oh god, I sound like Oprah.

"Well, it started with piano lessons."

"You're kidding," I say.

"No really, didn't you take piano lessons?"

I shake my head. "No, that's kind of like a rich person's sport. I did stuff that was free, you know, community soccer, Girl Scouts, stuff like that."

"You're lucky," he laughs. "It was torture, mainly for my teacher. Finally Mr. Leonard, that was my piano teacher, finally he told my parents that he just couldn't take their money anymore."

"Were they disappointed?" I kind of slide down on the mat so that we're level. It felt weird to be looking down at him.

"Probably, both of them are natural pianists. I guess it skipped a generation. But, the lessons did spark my love of music and they ultimately financed my vinyl buying habits."

"You mean albums?" I take a sip of my champagne.

"Yeah. There's some great stuff out there that can only be truly appreciated on vinyl. Anyway, when I finished college, they really pushed me to go on to law school. But I had already started this small label with a friend, so we made a deal. I told them that if the company didn't start going somewhere within a year, I'd go back to school. But if it did start to grow, well, they had to wish me well."

"So where are you in all that now?"

"Two years, growing, and I don't have to go back to school. What about you, what do you do?"

I just sit there. I'm not quite prepared for this question.

"Alex?"

"What do I do?" This question is like, one for grownups or something and I'm not sure how to answer it. "Well, I'm a student." I smile brightly and sip my champagne but my glass is empty so I end up swallowing air.

"Really?" he nods, seemingly intrigued. "Where are you going? What are you studying?"

Oh shit. He's staring right at me and I know I have to say something but definitely not the truth, so I go, "I'm just doing general studies, you know."

"Where?"

Shit. He's waiting for an answer and I'm totally trapped so I take a deep breath and I mention the name of the town that my high school is in. There's a state college there that goes by that name so I figure I'll just let him draw his own conclusions.

He knows something's up. I can tell by the way he's looking at me.

He leans in closer and goes, "How old are you?"

I'm sweating like a suspect on *NYPD Blue*. "Um, nineteen," I mumble.

"Nineteen? Is that even legal?"

"Legal for what?" I ask defensively, "Voting?" God, I'm lying by a year and a half as it is! "Well, how old are you?" I ask.

"Twenty-three."

"Oh, wow."

We just look at each other and then I start laughing. I do that when I get nervous.

Then Connor runs his hand down the length of my cheek and says, "Okay, I guess nineteen is a little young, but you happen to be nice and cute and I like hanging out with you. So maybe that cancels out the age difference?"

He's looking right at me and I can barely breathe. Then he leans in and starts kissing me and it's awesome and I just sort of follow his lead. I mean, it's not that I don't know how to kiss, I've been doing it since sixth grade, but since he's twenty-three, he's been doing it longer so I figure I could maybe learn something.

We kiss for a long time and I don't remember it ever being like this before. I can feel his fingers sliding inside the straps of my dress and pulling them down my shoulders. I'm not wearing a bra and part of me is thinking that I absolutely have to stop him, but the other part of me doesn't even try. He kisses me everywhere and I just lie back with my eyes closed, thinking I could do this forever.

He slides my dress all the way down to my waist and kisses my belly until he gets to my navel ring. He spins it between his fingers and says, "This is sexy."

I move my hands all over him. He's got a great body, muscular, but not too much, but I keep my hands mostly above the belt. It's not that I've never touched a penis before, because I have, but I just don't want to be the one to start that.

I'm not sure when, but at some point he has removed my dress and his jeans and now the only thing separating us is two cotton crotches. He starts moving south again and right when he's about to kiss me even lower, like way past my belly ring, I immediately sit up and shout, "*Stop!*" And then I feel like a total retard.

I cover my breasts with my hands and scramble for my dress. I can't even look at him, I feel so stupid. I'm some kinda nineteen year old.

He looks at me surprised and asks, "Are you okay?"

And I go, "I'm sorry but I can't do that. I'm menstruating." That's what I said. *Menstruating!* I sound like my sixth-grade health teacher. And I don't know why I said it because it's not even true. But it's just too soon for me, and there's no way I'm gonna tell him I'm a virgin. I pick up my dress from the floor and I'm just waiting for him to say, "Thank-you and good night."

But instead he looks at me and says, "It's okay. Really."

"It is?" I look at him suspiciously, unsure if he means it.

"Yeah, it's your call." He reaches down for his jeans and I watch him step into them, one leg at a time.

I'm standing in front of him half naked with my dress held tightly against me. I feel like such a loser, such a big baby. And no matter what he says I know I totally blew it. But it's too late now, it's not like I can take it back. I turn away from him and pull my dress over my head. When I face him again he's buttoning his shirt and smiling at me.

"You're not mad at me?" I venture.

He shakes his head. "Not at all. But I was wondering."

"What?"

"Well, how long will this take?"

"What?"

"I'm kidding." He looks at me and shrugs. "Well kind of."

I follow Connor outside and I'm just waiting for him to ditch me, to go in search of a more mature, accommodating girl, but instead he reaches for my hand, wraps his fingers around mine, and pulls me up alongside him.

Chapter 10

When we go back inside the house I'm surprised to find the party just as we left it. It seemed like we were in that cabana forever, like something monumental had happened. But now, seeing all these people slightly drunker, but basically unchanged, makes me feel like maybe it wasn't that big of a deal. I mean, Connor is still here, and I have every right to say no, right? I remember reading somewhere that your body is your temple and only you can choose who comes to worship. Whatever. All I know is that eventually I will lose this virginity of mine, but it's gonna be on my terms and it's gonna be glamorous.

We find M lounging on a giant-size beanbag chair, holding a drink in one hand, and a pool cue in the other. The room smells kind of weird like someone's been smoking pot or something but I'm sure it wasn't M 'cause neither one of us does stuff like that. When she sees me standing in the doorway she shouts, "Oh my god! I've been looking all over for you!"

I watch her struggle to get upright without spilling her drink. "Help me out here, would you?" she says.

I give her my hand and help her up. She rearranges her

Burberry plaid miniskirt that has risen up and twisted around, says hi to Connor and goes, "Hey Trevor come here, this is Alex."

I watch Trevor make his shot, and then scowl as he narrowly misses his pocket. He looks up and smiles and gives me a half-hearted wave. And I'm not sure if his lack of enthusiasm is because of the missed shot, or if he's already bored by me.

"I can't believe you missed that shot," Connor says, walking around the side of the pool table.

"I suppose you could do better?"

"You know it."

Connor looks around for a cue stick, and M goes, "Here, take mine, I'm bored with this game."

"We just started!" Trevor says.

"Yeah, well," M just shrugs and takes another sip of her drink.

I settle onto a velvet beanbag chair next to M and watch Connor and Trevor play pool, and I try to think of what celebrities they resemble. Trevor is kind of skinny and not very tall, with hair that's all dark roots and bleached tips. And with his dark brown eyes, and pale, English-schoolboy skin, he looks kind of like a guy version of Gwen Stefani. And Connor with his dark, wavy, tousled hair, swimming pool–blue eyes, hot body, and that one, slightly crooked, front tooth, makes me think of what Hugh Grant and Elizabeth Hurley's kid would have looked like if they hadn't broken up and she hadn't gotten knocked up by that other guy who thought he wasn't the dad but then it turned out he really was.

"Where were you guys?" M asks, giving me a suspicious look.

"We took a walk." I look at her briefly, then back at the guys.

"Where to?"

"Outside," I say, still not looking at her.

"Front or back?"

"Why?" I ask. I mean, god, she's practically leering at me.

"Because you're being so secretive that it makes me want to know."

"We were outside, in the back, in the cabana, by the pool. Okay? Happy now?" I look right at her.

"What were you doing in there?" She leans in and stares at me.

"Jeez, M!"

"Well?"

"Nothing, okay. Just talking." I fidget with the hem of my dress.

"Why so sensitive?" she asks.

I look over at Connor and Trevor, but they're into the game, they can't hear us. "Listen, we almost did it but then we didn't."

"Did you get coitus interrupted?" M laughs.

"Yeah, by me."

"What?"

"I just wasn't ready, I couldn't go through with it."

M looks at Connor who just made his shot and is pumping his arm into the air. "Well, he doesn't seem too upset about it. But I'm telling you, you really need to get it over with and put it behind you. You act like it's such a big deal, and it's really not."

I just look at M and shrug. Our realities are so different. She lost her virginity last summer to some hot surf instructor during a family vacation to Maui. She called me like the minute it was over to give me all the details. It's like, she just breezes through life never worried about the consequences. I wonder what it's like to always feel so safe.

"Well, there's one more thing," I tell her.

"What's that?"

"I told him I was nineteen," I whisper.

"*What?*" she shouts.

"Shhh." I look around frantically. "You heard me," I whisper.

"Does that make me nineteen too?"

"I guess."

"Cool." She takes a sip of her drink and leans back.

"What about you, what have you been doing?" I ask.

"Nothing. I watched that movie for a little while, then I bumped into Trevor and we've just been hanging out."

"Is there anyone famous here?"

"No, just a couple of Bachelorette wannabes." She sets down

her drink, then stands up and walks over to the pool table and leans against the far-left-corner pocket, the same one Connor is shooting for, only now he misses.

"Oh, and you almost had it," M says, giving him a flirty smile.

"I did have it. Until you distracted me," Connor says in a joking way, but I wonder if he's partly serious.

"Yeah, well you seem to be easily distracted," she says.

"What does that mean?" He leans his weight on his cue stick and looks at her, while Trevor lines up his next shot.

"Well, like how long did it take you to call Alex?"

Connor just stands there looking at her, and I'm sinking deeper and deeper into the beanbag chair, wondering where she's going with this and wishing she'd stop right now.

"Oh, that's right, you never did call her did you? See what I mean by easily distracted?"

M just stands there smiling and I'm completely frozen. I can't believe she just said that. I'm just about to say something, anything, when Connor goes, "Well, actually, I was waiting for Alex to call me. I thought that's how you do it in America. Lucky for me I found her in the hallway." Then he looks at me and smiles and winks and even though it was really nice of him to do that, I still want to kill her.

Then out of nowhere she goes, "Hey, is anybody else hungry? 'Cause, I'm starving. Do you think we could get some breakfast?"

"You want me to make you a waffle?" Trevor drops his stick and grabs her around the waist and nuzzles her ear. It's the second time he's seen her and he's already gone. It never fails.

"No, let's go somewhere," she says.

And so we leave all the guests to continue the party on their own, and pile into Trevor's Hummer and end up in some funky old diner with sticky, illustrated menus.

The restaurant scene is surreal. It's like being trapped in that Tori Amos video where she keeps morphing. The waitress looks like she's trying to morph into Christina Aguilera but that's not why I feel sorry for her. I mean, I can't imagine working here at this hour. Nothing but drunk people trying to sober up and not throw up before the long drive home.

When Connor slides in the booth next to me, he moves in so close that our legs are touching. He opens his menu and leans his shoulder into mine, and when I look up I catch M watching us with an expression I can't quite read.

Then Trevor picks up a menu and goes, "Okay, you guys just order anything you want, it's on me. But not you Connor, girls only, you're on your own."

So I go, "Well thanks, Trevor, but I think I'll just have coffee."

"No really, I mean it. You want this burger here," he holds up the menu and points at a picture of a greasy-looking burger, "You just say the word and I'll make it happen."

"Well, as generous as that offer is, I think I'll stick with coffee," I say.

"Okay, last call M, how 'bout it?"

"Well . . ."

So then the pseudo-Christina waitress comes over with her notepad, ready to take our order. I stick with coffee because every time I eat this late at night my dreams get even crazier than usual. Connor gets coffee and pancakes, Trevor taps his finger on the picture of the greasy burger and says, "This. I want this."

And M goes, "Okay. I'll start with a small garden salad with ranch dressing, on the side. Then I'd like a grilled cheese sandwich, but use very little butter please. I'd also like some peach cobbler warmed up with some vanilla ice cream, but if you could put the vanilla ice cream in a separate bowl, I'd appreciate it, because I don't like it when it gets all warm and runny. Oh, and a Diet Coke. Thank you."

The waitress doesn't even flinch. She just takes her tan, hair extensions, and notepad back into the kitchen to place our orders.

Trevor retrieves a pack of cigarettes from his shirt pocket and offers them all around, but Connor shakes his head and says, "Not me. I quit."

Trevor holds the pack in front of me and goes, "He'll never quit. We've been smoking forever."

I look at Connor and he just shrugs, then I push the pack away because M and I don't smoke. Not to mention that it's illegal to smoke in restaurants in California and I wish that Trevor would just stop because I'm kind of a wuss about rules like that. But then M grabs the pack from Trevor pulls one out, taps it on the table like a professional smoker, and holds it up to her mouth, waiting for a light.

I look at her totally shocked because we gave up smoking after three tries in junior high when we realized it didn't make us look cool, it just made us smell bad. But now Trevor gives her a light and she's smoking it, and I can't believe she's doing that but I don't say anything.

When our food arrives M and Trevor finally put out their cigarettes and everybody just sort of digs in. There isn't much in the way of conversation, which is fine by me 'cause I sort of shut down when I get tired and it's hard for me to act all vivacious. Trevor and M are sharing off each other's plates and whispering back and forth. Then suddenly they both get up and say, "We'll be right back."

I watch M walk away and wonder what they're up to. Normally she'd drag me into the bathroom with her so we could talk about the guys and stuff. But I guess she's not going in there with Trevor so they can have a conversation.

I take a sip of my coffee and lean my head back and close my eyes. I feel Connor squeeze my hand and then lean over and kiss me softly on the cheek. I open my eyes and smile at him.

About fifteen minutes later Trevor and M come back and want to go. She's acting all hyper and fidgety and weird, and when I try to catch her eye she purposely looks away. And I'm really starting to wonder what went on in the bathroom just now. I figured she probably went in there to fool around with Trevor, but now I'm thinking there was more to it, like maybe they were doing drugs or something. I mean, earlier, when she was playing pool and the room smelled like pot, I was so positive it wasn't her. But now watching her act all strange and secretive, I'm no longer sure.

When we walk outside I'm surprised to find that it's still dark. I mean, it feels like it should be the next afternoon or something. But technically it's Saturday morning and I remember that I'm scheduled to open the store today.

"So where to now?" M asks bouncing up and down in the backseat of the Hummer.

"Wherever you want." Trevor looks at her from the rearview mirror and smiles.

"Alex, what do you think?"

I look at my watch and then I look at everyone else, and I don't want to be a major party wrecker but I really need to get back to Orange County so I can sleep, shower, and change before work. "Well, I hate to say it, but um, I really have to go home soon." There I said it, peer pressure be damned.

"No!" M whines. "The night is young!"

I look at her and I can't believe she's whining like that, but I just say, "I'm sorry, but I have to work tomorrow."

"Call in sick!" She rolls her eyes, clearly frustrated with me, which just makes me more determined.

"I'm sorry, I can't. I can't call in sick." I'm glaring at her and I feel really embarrassed to be fighting like this in front of Connor.

"Well, I'm not going home, Alex. So just take these, take the car."

She's dangling her car keys in front of me and I can't believe she's doing this, but I just swipe them out of her hand and say, "Well what about you, how are you getting home?"

"Don't you worry about me, I'll find a way." She gives me a smug look and I'm so mad I just stare out the window for the rest of the ride.

When we get back to Trevor's, Connor gets out of the Hummer and M climbs into the front seat and slams the door between us. She waves at me as they drive away, and I cannot believe she's ditching me like this.

"Are you going to be okay?" Connor asks. "I know it's a long drive."

I give him a smile I don't really own and say, "Yeah, I'll be fine. I'll just listen to some music."

Then he kisses me good-bye and he tastes like pancakes and maple syrup and it's really hard to stop.

Chapter 11

On Monday morning I pull into the student lot and look around for M's car, partly because we usually park next to each other and partly because I'm wondering if she's here yet since I haven't talked to her since she ditched me on Saturday night.

I tried calling her yesterday after I got home from work but her mom answered the phone. I could hear her go, "Hello? Hello?" and then "Who is this?" and that's when I hung up. I know that's a terrible thing to do, but I didn't feel like talking to her and I couldn't figure out why she was in M's room answering her private line. I spent the rest of the night hoping she wouldn't star sixty-nine me.

But since M wasn't in French or Calculus, or even at our lunch tree, I'm starting to worry that maybe something happened to her, like maybe she didn't get home safely, and that makes me feel guilty about being mad at her.

I switch books at my locker and run to my English class because I don't want to be late and attract any unnecessary attention. When I get to the door, I look around for M but she's not here either, so I just sort of slink to my desk and hope for the best.

Mr. Sommers walks in, glances at us briefly, then goes over to his desk where he starts flipping through some papers and rubbing his scraggly beard in a distracted way. And I'm thinking, well today must be the day. The day when he finally hands back those *Anna K* papers, the one I still haven't started. He'll look at me when the papers have all been handed out and then he'll say in front of the entire class, "Alex, I need to speak to you later." And then everyone will turn around and snicker at the former-homecoming-princess-now-big-loser sitting in the next-to-last row.

I watch him get up from his desk clutching some paper in one hand and still fingering his beard with the other. He's standing in front of us and he's looking right at me with these dark eyes that look like they've seen things he's not going to tell you about in this AP English class. And as much as I want to look away I can't, because part of me is just like all the others. Part of me wants to watch this train wreck that is surely headed my way.

He clears his throat like he always does at the beginning of class and I sink a little lower in my seat, preparing for a verbal caning, when he says, "I'd like to read you a story written by one of my students that really impressed me."

So I relax. I'm relieved that it's not about me and I wonder why I've become so paranoid. Then he starts reading "Holly Would," that short story I turned in instead of the Tolstoy paper. I sit frozen at my desk. I can't even believe it.

When he's finished reading someone goes, "Who wrote that? Whose was that? That was really good."

And then Mr. Sommers looks at me and waits and in an unsure voice I say, "I wrote it?"

And then everyone turns around and stares at me in disbelief. And then someone who I used to dismiss, someone who once felt like a total loser because of me, someone who is now well aware of my social decline, says, "No way. No way, she wrote that."

And now everyone is staring at me to see how I'll respond.

But I don't say anything because I remember how I once treated this person and how it always comes back to you.

Mr. Sommers sits on the edge of his desk and says, "Alex did indeed write it and it got me thinking. For your next assignment I'd like you to write a short story, fifteen-hundred words, due Monday."

I sit up straighter, feeling good about myself in a classroom for the first time in two years. No homework for me! I've got plenty more where that came from, a whole drawer full of stories that I've written, and they're not all about Richard Branson either. But it's just a little hobby of mine. I mean, it's not serious or anything.

Christine the Collector raises her hand and asks, "Mr. Sommers what should the story be about?"

And he goes, "This is a creative exercise. It can be about anything you want. Just use your imagination."

She pushes her headband back an invisible inch then looks at Mr. Sommers and goes, "I was wondering if it's possible to get an alternate assignment?"

Now the whole class is staring at her and her eyes are all red, and she looks like she's gonna cry or something.

He gives her a concerned look and says, "Christine, relax. Just try to have fun with it. Get creative."

And then, get this, she says, "But I don't know how to be creative."

And I just look at her and give her the smirk I've been holding in for the last two years because that's the most pathetic statement I've ever heard.

Mr. Sommers just shrugs and says, "Do your best." Then he hands me my story, and gives everyone else their graded Tolstoy papers.

And right there, in red ink, in the upper-left-hand corner, is an A. I just stare at it for the longest time. I haven't received a letter from that far north in the alphabet in like two years. He also wrote a note at the bottom saying something like, even if I didn't write what was assigned, he's glad that I chose to write, and to write well.

And even though that makes me feel really good for a change, it also makes me feel guilty. Like now I seriously have to write that *Anna K* paper.

Chapter 12

On my way home from school I decide to stop in at my dad's office. I mean, he's really left me with no choice since he refuses to return my calls. Besides, I'm feeling pretty good about the A I just got, and since good moments in my life tend to be pretty fleeting, I figure I better strike while I'm hot, right?

I pull into the lot and park right next to a brand new, shiny, black Porsche that I know belongs to my father since he would never allow another mortal to park in his reserved space. And I consider this a good sign because if he can afford a Porsche he can certainly pay my way through college.

I stare at my reflection in the rearview mirror and try to muster the courage to face him. The last time I came here was over a year ago when I had to beg for my child-support check, and I left empty-handed. I try to summon one good memory, just one decent moment we might have shared when I was a kid, just a little something to get me through this meeting. But the truth is he really wasn't around much and the few times he was, well, it's not worth remembering.

I run my hands through my hair, recheck my lip gloss, and climb out of my car. I may be quaking with fear inside, but I walk with intent and purpose just in case someone is watching from a distant window. And when I push through the double glass doors with the words Sky Investments etched on them, I wonder why he's always so reluctant to invest in me.

I stand in front of the modern, steel reception desk waiting to see who it will be this time. Every time I come to his office there's a new secretary. I mean, he changes them almost as often as he changes girlfriends.

"Can I help you?" A skinny, Clairol blonde, with an abundant chest walks down the hallway and slides around the other side of the desk. She's wearing an outfit that would normally be paired with a thick, black bar across the eyes and the word, DON'T! in red capital letters and extreme punctuation overhead.

"I'm here to see my dad." I look directly at her and fight the urge to fidget.

She looks me over, then in a condescending tone asks, "And who might that be?"

I narrow my eyes and say, "My dad is Brad Sky, the President of Sky Investments. Your boss. Can I see him now?"

Her expression instantly changes to one of curiosity and caution. "Oh. Okay. And your name please?"

"Alex."

I watch her pick up the phone, push a button, and in an intimate tone that tells me they've slept together says, "There's an Alex here? She says she's your daughter? I didn't know you had a daughter. Oh, all right." Then she looks at me and gestures, "Go right in."

When I open the door he's waiting on the other side. "Alex!" He says, "What a wonderful surprise!"

He's acting all happy to see me and tries to give me a big hug. I let him grab hold of me for about half a second, then I duck out of it and settle into the cracked, brown-leather club chair across from his desk.

"What brings you here?" he asks, his face clad in his deal-closing smile and a pair of trendy titanium glasses that are resting on the bridge of his nose.

I watch him ease into his executive chair on the other side of the desk, then I look around the office walls, at the framed degrees and certificates, and that stupid Nagel print he bought in the eighties and refuses to take down. College degrees, schlock art, but not one picture of my sister or me. It's like we've ceased to exist in this new, postdivorce world he created for himself.

I face him and say, "You haven't returned my calls so I decided to visit."

"What? I didn't know you called." He runs his hand through his salt-and-pepper Richard Gere–style hair and gestures toward the general vicinity of the reception desk, "Cheri must have forgotten to give me the message."

"I called you at home dad." I look right at him. "Did you say her name was Cherry?" I ask incredulously.

"So what can I do for you?" he asks, ignoring my question.

I take a deep breath and clasp my hands in my lap so I won't fidget, then I look directly at him and just say it. "I need your help."

He looks at me with controlled panic, adjusts his pastel, silk tie that color coordinates with his light pink shirt, and charcoal gray pin-striped suit, and nods. "Okay, what kind of help?"

"Financial help." I glance down at my lap and see that I'm squeezing my hands together so tightly that my knuckles are white.

"Okay, okay." He's bobbing his head up and down like he does when he's thinking up a good exit strategy. "What do you need it for? A new prom dress?"

"A prom dress?" I shake my head. Is he kidding? "What? You think I drove here because of a prom dress? I'm not living in Dawson's fucking Creek Dad."

"Watch your language!" he shouts.

I roll my eyes and shake my head. I know I shouldn't have used the *f* word, but I can't believe him. He doesn't even know me! I try to center myself, and calm down, because getting mad never works with him. So I take a deep breath and start over. "Dad, no, I'm not going to the prom, okay? My life isn't really like that anymore. I need money for my future, you know? So I can have one?"

He locks eyes with me for a second, then reaches into his desk drawer for his checkbook, and his big, important, Montblanc pen. Then he writes out a check for five hundred dollars. "Will this help?" he asks, holding it up so I can see it.

I look at the money he's offering and I can't believe it. That barely covers one month's child support. I lean back in my chair and say, "Are you joking?"

He drops the check on the desk between us and says, "Well, how much are we talking here Alex?"

"I need to know if you're going to pay for college." I wipe my sweaty palms onto my jeans.

"Have you applied?"

"Yes." I look directly at him and hold his gaze.

"And were you accepted?"

"Yes. Into one." He doesn't need to know it was on a contingent basis.

I watch him rock back in his chair and regard me from over the top of his trendy glasses. "Have you asked your mother for help?"

"Are you kidding? She works like a dog just to pay the mortgage you stuck her with!"

He takes on a smug expression and says, "She should have sold while the market was hot. I told her."

Five years later and he's still judging her. I just can't take it anymore. "And you should have paid your alimony and child support like the judge ordered!" I shout. "Look, she won't go after you, and this is not easy for me either, but I really need your help. Please. I'm not kidding. This is my life. It's not a joke." I look across the desk at him and I can't believe it's come to this. I can't believe I'm begging.

He looks at me completely unaffected and says, "Now is not a good time."

"What?" I say. "Not a good time? I saw your new Porsche outside! That's four years at a state school just sitting in your parking space!"

He shakes his head and gestures to a stack of papers on his desk, "It's not like you think. You see this? All bills. The Porsche? It's leased. I just can't help you right now."

I look at the check lying on the desk between us and then I lock eyes with him. When he's the first to look away, I stand up. I grab the door handle then turn back and look at his stupid pink shirt, his crappy art, and his greedy face. I don't know why I expected anything different.

When I open the door Cheri is standing right there but I don't start crying until I'm safely inside my car.

Chapter 13

W hen I get home my mom has set the table for two, which is kind of surprising since we rarely eat together and I'm guessing this must be because of the conference at school the other day. I look at her tentatively since I don't know what to expect. I mean, I know she hasn't been too pleased with me lately.

"Hi," she says, pouring a big pot full of pasta into one of those draining bowls with all the holes. "I'm glad you're home, I made spaghetti."

I walk over to where she stands and check out the steaming noodles. "You made spaghetti? Really?" I throw my stuff on the counter and sit at the table and let her serve me a plate full of pasta. "What's the occasion?" I ask.

"I just thought maybe we could spend some time together. We haven't had a chance to really talk since our meeting with Mrs. Gross. So how've you been?" She passes me the grated Parmesan cheese and looks at me expectantly.

"Fine," I lie. She doesn't need to know about my dad.

She nods her head then says, "I saw M's mother in the grocery store the other day."

"M's mom goes to the grocery store?" I ask, taking a bite of my pasta.

My mom covers her mouth and says, "No, I don't think she does. She made it clear she was just on her way home from yoga and needed a bottle of water."

"Did you tell her that you were just on your way home from work and needed a week's worth of groceries?"

She just shrugs. "We didn't talk long." And then she looks at me and her eyes grow darker when she asks, "So how's school going Alex? Do you need any help? Anything you want to talk about?"

"No, I'm doing better," I say, and I'm surprised to realize that it's actually true, well for today anyway. "My English teacher liked a short story I wrote and he read it out loud to the class."

"Really?"

"Yeah, and he gave me an A too." I break off a piece of garlic bread and drag it along the top of my pasta, caking it with red sauce.

"I used to do a little writing," she says. "But one day your father made fun of one of my stories so I stopped."

She cuts a meatball in half with her fork and looks at me closely, and all I can think is, *Here-we-go.* I take a drink of my water and look down at my plate, waiting for the retelling of her favorite story, the one about how he wrecked her life.

But instead she says, "So you're studying creative writing?"

I look at her surprised, but I just say, "Not really, We just finished reading *Anna Karenina.* Have you read it?"

She nods. "Years ago, when I was your age. She gets hit by a train or something, right?"

"Yeah, something like that."

"Do you have to write a paper on it?"

She's looking right at me and I hate lying to her so I just go, "Um, yeah, I do." And then the phone rings and I practically jump through a hoop of fire to get it.

It's my sister calling from New York. She moved there right after she graduated college, and she has this totally cool job as an editor with a major fashion magazine. They don't pay as much as you'd think and New York is like a totally expensive place to live, but I really do admire her. Her whole life just seems really glamorous. She has a studio apartment in a place called SoHo which stands for something I can't remember, but it's supposed to be really hip. And she has this boyfriend that she showed me a picture of once and he looked really cute. His eyes were sort of squinted closed, but she said that's because it was taken in the sun at the beach in the Hamptons. That's supposed to be some chichi place in the East.

"Hey, Alex, how are you?" she asks.

"Okay, how's New York?"

"Bad weather, very crowded, terribly exciting. I still love it here."

"Yeah, I still love it here too."

"I'll bet." She laughs. "So what's new?"

And even though I promised myself I wouldn't tell anyone what happened today, I just can't keep it in, so I go, "Dad just leased a new Porsche, has a girlfriend named Cherry, and he's not paying for me to go to college."

"What?" she asks, all the way from Manhattan. "Are you serious?"

I look at my mother who is staring at me, straining to hear both sides of the conversation, and suddenly I feel bad about mentioning his stupid girlfriend. I didn't mean to make my mom feel bad. I turn and face the wall and even though she can still hear me I say, "Well, he wouldn't return my calls so I ambushed him at his office. He says he's broke and can't do it. But I don't believe him."

"I don't believe him either. Oh Alex, I'm sorry."

"It's not your fault," I say.

"Can I help in any way?"

"No, but I'll let you know how it all turns out." I look at my mom. She's practically falling out of her chair. "I think Mom wants to talk to you."

I hand the phone to my mother and start clearing my plate. I wished I hadn't said anything, and just kept it to myself because my mom is going to ask me all the details now and I don't feel like talking about it anymore. It is what it is and there's nothing I can do about it. I mean, I can't force him to care about me.

Sure enough, she hangs up the phone and says, "What was that I heard about you going to your father's office today?"

I pour some dish soap onto a damp sponge and say, "Nothing. Don't worry about it."

She turns in her chair until she's facing me and says, "Well I am worried about it because it obviously upset you and I'd like to know what happened."

"Really?" I look at her. The wet, soapy plate I'm holding is dripping onto the floor. "Do you really want to know about it because it upset me? Or because you just want to know about him?" It's a terrible thing to say, especially when I saw her eyes right after I said it. But it's out there now and I can't take it back.

"What is that supposed to mean?"

I finish rinsing the plate and say, "Plenty of things upset me, Mom, but you never want to know about them unless it involves Dad."

"That's not true!"

"It is true. You never ask me how I am."

"How can you say that? I even went to your school!"

"You showed up only because Mrs. Gross called you at work and guilted you into it. And then you kept looking at your watch, the whole time. You have no idea what it's like for me, and you never bother to ask." I shake my head and reach for a dish towel.

"Well maybe you have no idea what it's like for me."

"How could I *not* know?" I'm yelling now, but I just don't care. "You remind me every chance you get! It's been five solid years of living in the past. He's *gone* Mom, and you've still got a drawer full of his stuff in your bedroom. He doesn't pay alimony, he doesn't pay child support, but you don't do a damn thing about it because you'd rather just sit back and suffer and talk about how it's all his fault."

"He let me down!" She looks a little shaky when she says it and I know I've really upset her, but I'm a little upset too.

"Yeah, well, he let me down too! He was my only shot at college but he won't pay for it, so now I can't go. He left both of us, Mom, not just you." I throw the dish towel on the counter and face her.

She gives me a long look and I know I've gone too far, so I turn around and busy myself at the sink. I've got my back to her when I hear her say, "I had dreams too you know."

"Whatever." I roll my eyes and shake my head and put the dry plate in the cupboard overhead.

"If I had it to do over again—"

There's no way I'm going to listen to the rest of that. What, so I can hear her say she wouldn't have had me if she had it to do over again? No thanks. Being ditched by one parent is enough for today. So I turn around and face her and put my hand in the air and say, "Just stop. I don't want to hear anymore."

She looks at me and shakes her head and says, "I don't know why you thought you could count on him. I don't know what gave you that idea."

I grab my backpack and sling it over my shoulder and look at her and say, "I guess I just wanted to believe that he really did care about me. But don't worry. Now I know better." Then I leave the kitchen before she can say anything else.

Chapter 14

The next day at school I see M walking across the quad talking on her cell phone. When she sees me she runs over and goes, "Say hi to Trevor!"

I grab the phone she's thrusting in my face and go, "Hi Trevor," then I hand it back and walk toward my locker.

I'm standing in front of it, trying to remember the combination, when M comes over and goes, "Oh my god! Did you see Tiffany's sling? What a faker! Did you see it?"

"I didn't even notice."

"How could you miss it? It's freakin' furry zebra striped!"

"Yeah?" I finally get my locker open. I grab a handful of textbooks I have no intention of reading and put them in my backpack.

M's still going on about Tiffany but I'm not listening. Finally she looks at me and goes, "Are you okay?"

I slam my locker shut, look right at her, and go, "No. I guess I'm not."

"Well what's wrong?"

"In case you didn't notice, you totally ditched me at that party."

"I didn't ditch you. You had to go home and I wasn't ready, so I gave you the keys. What's the damage?"

"I just didn't think it was cool."

"Are you serious?" She looks at me in shock and it makes me wonder if I'm overreacting. "I'm sorry, really. I guess I got a little caught up."

I just shrug and start walking toward class and she follows me. "What happened to you yesterday?" I look over at her. "How come you weren't at school?"

"I was home sick." She looks away.

"What'd you have?"

She stops in front of the door and whispers, "A massive hangover. I didn't get in until Sunday night and like, my mom was already home. It was a serious close call."

"You were at Trevor's that whole time?"

"We went *everywhere*. It's like he knows every cool person, and every cool place in LA. You wouldn't even believe the stuff we did." She shakes her head and looks around the campus. "God, this place is such a dump. It totally sucks being stuck here after a weekend like that."

"Did you sleep with him?" I ask, figuring she did, but still wanting to know.

"Yeah, and it was completely amazing. I think I'm in love."

She gives me a searching look but I don't say anything. I'm starting to feel like I'm falling further and further behind in the maturity race, and soon I won't be able to catch up.

"Anyway, by the time I got home I looked pretty bad, and I didn't expect my mom to be home. I thought they were at some doctor's conference, but apparently she decided not to go 'cause she's leaving for some spa or something instead. So, I hope you don't mind but I told her I was at your house."

"Whatever," I say.

"I'm sorry if you felt like I ditched you, really. I just thought it was a good solution. I didn't mean to hurt your feelings."

She's giving me this sad look and I decide to just let it go. "Okay, forget it. You know I tried calling you but your mom answered."

"She did? Shit!"

"Yeah, it was weird."

"What did you say? Did you talk to her?" M looks panicked.

"I didn't say anything. I hung up."

"No way!"

"Way. But I felt bad about it afterwards."

"I wonder what the hell she was doing in my room?"

"Who knows," I say. "I've got bigger issues right now anyway."

"Like what?"

I look at her and shake my head. I feel like I'm on the verge of tears but I hold it back with all my might. "I had it out with my dad last night. I went to his office. He's not paying for college, end of story." I move away from the door so some of my classmates can get in, and then I wipe my nose with the back of my hand and continue. "Lets face it, my grades are crap, I can't swing a scholarship, and the only school that did accept me did so on a contingent basis, only if I could get my grades up, but now even if I do, I still can't afford it. So I guess it's just not gonna happen for me."

"Well, you could always get a loan or something."

"Yeah, whatever." She's looking at me with pity and I just can't take it. "Listen," I push past her, "I have to go to the bathroom. I'll see you in class," I say. But as soon as I'm around the corner I beeline for the parking lot and get in my car.

I check my wallet. I just got paid so I've got three crumbled twenties, a fresh ten, a stained five, and two crisp ones. And since I filled up recently I should have enough gas to get me to LA and back.

Only my car won't start. I turn the key in the ignition, nothing. I turn the key and bang on the steering wheel, nothing. I turn the key and bang on the steering wheel and scream every bad word I know, and still, nothing.

Well, that's just great. The bell rang like five minutes ago and if I go to class now I'll get in trouble for being tardy. And if I'm gonna get in trouble then I may as well go all the way and get in trouble for truancy. So I sit in my turquoise blue Karmann Ghia and start crying. And after a few minutes of that, I wipe my nose on my sleeve and look in the rearview mirror and I look even worse than I imagined. So I grab a faded, red bandanna from the glove compartment, spit on it, and wipe the supposedly water-proof mascara from my cheeks. I know it sounds gross, but what was I supposed to do?

So then, just to be a glass-half-full kinda girl, I turn the key again, and the engine starts. So now that I look like crap, with makeup and saliva smeared across my face, my car decides to take me to LA. That's the kind of karma I have.

I've never been to LA by myself, and it feels a little weird to be navigating the freeways alone. But the sun is shining hot and bright and I roll both windows down so I can feel the wind rushing around me, almost like in M's convertible. And even though my car is an old clunker, it's got a really great stereo system that I saved up for. So I insert that Nelly Furtado CD that I love, the one that has that song about being like a bird and flying away, and since I know all the words to all the songs I sing along at the top of my lungs, all the way to LA. And it feels really good to be young and free like this. It's almost like with each spin of my wheels, I get farther and farther from my troubles. Like I can just drive straight into my future and leave all the bad stuff behind.

I go to the sandwich shack. I'm not even hungry but it's what we always do. When the cute guy behind the counter sees me, he gets all happy and looks immediately to my right, then left, then over my shoulder, frantically searching for M.

"It's just me today." I shrug, and he definitely looks disappointed. "Um, can I get a bottle of water?"

"Yeah. Hey, how's your friend?" He's trying to act nonchalant, but just asking about her has got him all lit up.

"She's fine. She's perfect." I give him a dollar fifty, then I go find a place to sit.

The same old cast of characters is out today, the hippie girl who sells colorful, blown-glass bongs, the creepy magician with the extra-long sleeves, and those fake henna tattoo people. I did that once like a year ago. The actual tattoo faded in a day, but the tribal band lived on in the form of a nasty rash for about a month.

I sit on the concrete bench and close my eyes and enjoy the warmth of the sun beating down on me.

I'm in Marrakech. The desert heat is unrelenting, but I'm dressed for it in a breezy, sheer, caftan, and those little pointy slippers that are made here in Morocco. My hair is pulled back into a complicated twist, and my eyes are shielded by my celebrity-size, shiny, black, Chanel sunglasses. I rise from my luxurious divan and walk out into the courtyard. I remove my caftan and let it fall to the ground, revealing my perfect nakedness. Some of the houseboys stop working and stare, but I ignore them, as I walk to the edge of the pool and dive in a perfect arc. I glide underwater to the other side, where Connor is waiting . . .

When I open my eyes that crazy iguana man is standing right in front of me, blocking my rays. Jeez, he's like the cruelest reality check imaginable.

"Wanna pet the iguana?" He smiles at me, but his pupils look crazy.

"Um, no thanks." I try to scoot back without being too obvious about it. He has a weird smell.

"It's just two dollars," he says.

"What's just two dollars?"

"To pet the iguana!" He's practically yelling at me now.

"Um, yeah, well, no thanks. I really don't want to pet him." I take a sip of my water and look around nervously.

"Suit yourself," he gives me a look like I'm missing out on a huge opportunity and turns to walk away.

And even though he creeps me out, now that he's leaving I'm reluctant to let him go, so I say, "Can I ask you a question?"

"Maybe." He looks at me expectantly.

"What do you do?"

"What?" He squints at me and his eyes contain so much red I can't tell what color they're supposed to be.

"I mean, I see you here all the time and I'm wondering what it is that you do. Do you work here?"

"Yeah, yeah, I work here." He raises his eyebrows and smiles.

"Well, where do you work?" I ask. I really am curious.

He starts pointing and twirling, "Where do I work?" he says. "Right here, and over there, and down there, and back there. I distribute happiness."

"You what?" I give him a skeptical look.

"I *distribute happiness!*" he says it slowly like I'm the moron, not him.

"You mean, by letting people pet your lizard?"

"That's one way." He nods, seemingly pleased that I'm catching on.

"Are *you* happy?" I don't know why, but I feel like I have to know.

"Happier than you," he says.

"How would you know?"

"Because you're lost, and I'm not." He says this with such certainty, that it really pisses me off.

"Yeah well, you never leave the boardwalk, so how could you get lost?" I give him an ugly look.

He shakes his head. "You've got to find your way, before it's too late."

"Oh yeah, like you did? I mean, where do you live?" I look down at his disgusting, bare feet. "And where are your shoes?" I don't know why but he's making me feel really defensive.

He looks down at his thick, nasty, yellow toenails and laughs. "Life is a journey. This is mine."

He's standing there laughing but I can tell he pities me. The iguana man feels sorry for *me!* I finish my water and stand up carefully, because I don't want him to see how much he's upsetting me. "Okay, well, nice meeting you," I say, waving my hand in the air.

And as I'm walking away I hear him yell, "We're not so different you know. You and me, we're the same!"

When I get to my car I lock the door and grip the steering wheel and try to calm down. I scan my side- and rearview mirrors watching him wandering aimlessly, up and down the boardwalk. He walks the same walk every day, the miles just adding up but he's always here. He's putting all his effort into going nowhere. And I wonder if he's right. If we really are the same. Like, maybe that will be me someday, some big, weirdo, lizard chick, wearing a fake Versace suit and stilettos, with some funky reptile shitting all over my shoulder. It's so hard for me to imagine my future that it seems like a real possibility.

I shake my head and refuse to think like this any longer. Then I dig my cell phone out of my purse and call Connor. The moment he answers I panic and nearly hang up.

"Hello?"

"Hey, Connor? It's Alex."

"Alex, hey. What's going on?"

"Um, nothing. Um, well, it's just that I'm in LA and I thought I'd call and say hey." Oh god, I sound like a total retard.

"You're in LA? Are you with M?"

"No, it's just me."

"Brilliant! Why don't you come by?"

"Now?"

"Well, no. Not now. I'm wrapping up a little business. How 'bout in a couple hours, say around six?"

"Okay."

"Listen, even better. Meet me at Harry's. Do you know where it is?"

"Yes," I lie. I think it's in Santa Monica but I'm really not sure, and I don't want him to know that I don't know, 'cause Harry's is one of those places where you're just supposed to know where it is.

"Great, we can grab some dinner then go see this band I might sign."

"Okay, Harry's at six." I look at my watch. I've got three hours to figure out where it is.

I put my car in reverse and glance at myself in the rearview mirror. I really need to find a makeup counter.

So I go to the LA location of the store where I work 'cause all I have to do is show my employee ID card and I can get a 20 percent discount. When I walk in I go right past the girls in those creepy white lab coats, past the ones caked in overpriced French makeup, and straight for those club kids working behind the cool counter.

I plop myself onto some tall awkward stool, smile at the Marilyn Manson wannabe wielding a powder brush and say, "Help!"

"Hmmmm." He holds my face up to the most unforgiving light and asks, "So what are your makeup goals?"

Goals? Is he kidding? I don't even have life goals, much less cosmetic ones. "Well," I begin, "I need to look nineteen, and I need to look way better than I do right now. Maybe a little like Gisele Bundchen? Is that possible?"

He purses his lips and shakes his head. "Gisele? Negative. I'm thinking for you a combination Betty Paige meets Liv Tyler."

"Have at it!" I say facing the light again.

One hour and several layers of makeup later, the only thing Betty, Liv, and I have in common is dark hair and a smoky eye pencil he swore he once sold to Liv's dad. But I scraped all my money together anyway and bought the pencil, the lipstick, and some powder, and now I have just enough left over for some new underwear.

I need the new underwear because I've decided I'm going to sleep with Connor. I figure if I'm gonna be a bad girl and ditch school, then I may as well be a really bad girl and lose my virginity. I mean, I think I'm finally ready. I pretty much know what to expect.

One day, back in like, fifth grade, I was peeking around my house, looking for some lost earring. I was really tearing the place apart, looking under beds, inside cupboards, everything. Well, under my parent's bed I found some creepy sex book. You know, the illustrated, how-to kind with captions and hairy armpits? I read that thing from cover to cover, trying to ignore how ugly the participants were drawn. I mean, I committed that book to memory, and it's a good thing too, because once, after the divorce, I went looking for it and it was gone. Either my dad took it with him, covertly stashing it under his arm, or my mom threw it out, vowing to never, ever, have that sort of illustrated sex again.

So I end up with a black lacy thong, which is a far cry from my usual pastel florals that my mom buys for me in three-packs. In the trunk of my car is a strapless black dress and some high-heeled sling backs that belong to M. So I go back to the parking lot, grab my stuff and take it into the department store bathroom and change. When I walk out of the stall I swear I don't look anything like the virginal, truant, high school senior that I am. Then I dial four-one-one on my cell phone and get the address to this Harry's place.

Chapter 15

Well, it's not in Santa Monica like I thought so I'm really glad that I didn't mention that to Connor. It's in Century City, which is a part of town that I'm not too familiar with because it's mostly all corporate and stuff so there's really no reason for me to ever go there.

So I'm driving down Century Boulevard and I'm wondering how long it will be before the school sends a cut card to my house, and if I'll be able to retrieve it before my mom can get her hands on it. And then I wonder why I even care if she sees it since there's not much she can do about it anyway. I mean, I can't see how it really matters since I can't go to college now because of my grades and my dad and all.

But you know what? Screw college! I mean, maybe I really, like deep down inside, maybe I don't really want to go. Maybe that's why I've been carrying on like this, you know, so like, there'd be no choice to make. And who says I have to go anyway? Who made that rule? Plenty of people have skipped out on college and have done really well. For instance, look at Richard Branson! He didn't even make it out of high school and look what he's done! He's worth billions of dollars and has even been knighted by the Queen of England (which means people *have* to call him

Sir). And now that I'm hanging out with Connor and stuff, I'm gonna get all the real-life connections and experience that you can't get from some stupid college dorm room or textbook. I mean, think of all the big-time people Connor probably knows from being in the music industry on two different continents. And who knows where that will lead? The chances of ending up somewhere really great are almost guaranteed, and I'll probably even get there faster than all those losers who waste four good years and more going to school.

When I see the sign for Harry's I pull over and park on the street because I don't have much cash on me and I don't want to waste whatever's left on valet parking.

I walk into a room that's so dim it takes a minute for my eyes to adjust. The bar looks just like it did in the picture I saw in a "Hip Hangouts" article in *Instyle* magazine, all dark wood and big mirrors. I don't see Connor anywhere, but I grab an empty stool and squint at the multicolored chalkboard drink menu. They have like fifty different kinds of beer but I don't want to order that because it makes me bloated, and naked and bloated is not a good combination. I don't know enough about wine to even attempt that, so I think about playing it safe and just ordering a club soda with lime, but then I catch a glimpse of myself in the large mirror on the wall in front of me, and I don't know if it's the dim lighting or what, but I decide on a cosmopolitan. I've never actually had one before, but if it's good enough for the cast of *Sex and the City* it's good enough for me. I mean, I'm wearing new makeup and a thong, surely I can pull this off.

So when the bartender says in an English accent, "Can I help you?"

I go, "I'll have a cosmopolitan, please."

Then he looks at me closely and says, "I'll need to see your ID."

And I break out in an immediate sweat. I guess there's a big difference between faking nineteen and faking twenty-one. He's giving me this all-knowing stare as I unzip my Hello Kitty purse, which right now looks not at all hip but entirely juvenile. As I'm fishing around for my matching Hello Kitty wallet my hands are shaking and I'm contemplating whether I should really go through with this, or just ditch this plan and order a Shirley Temple, when Connor walks up and goes, "Alex! You look brilliant!" And then he hugs me and kisses me and says, "I see you've met Simon." And then he slaps hands with the bartender and says, "Bring me a beer, and get Alex anything she wants." Then he puts his arm around me and goes, "I've got us a booth in the corner."

I don't relax until I'm safely seated in the booth with a menu on my plate and a cosmopolitan on the table in front of me. Then I make a mental note to trash this cartoon purse first thing tomorrow.

"So what brings you to the neighborhood?" Connor leans on the table and takes a sip of his beer.

I'm prepared for this question, so I say, "Well, I was up here for a meeting. Um, you know, with a professor. From my college." Shit, that did not sound convincing.

"And how was your meeting?" He looks at me and waits.

"It went very well." I nod my head and smile and try to look directly at him without blinking so I'll appear more honest. "What about you? How was your day?" It's better if he talks since I'm just not pulling this off like I thought I could.

"My day was brilliant. Everything is coming together. But I can't go into all the details just yet, it's early still, and I don't want to jinx it." He winks at me.

"Oh." I nod my head and smile and take another sip of my drink. It's sweeter than I imagined, and I'm not sure if I like it, but I feel like I should finish it after all I went through to get it.

So when the waitress brings our fish and chips I look down at my plate and I'm disappointed to see that everything is beige. And I'm not even sure if I like fish and chips, but it's what you're supposed to get at Harry's so that's what we ordered. I watch Connor reach for some weird liquid stuff with a familiar scent and sprinkle it all over his food.

"What's that?" I ask, hoping this question won't make me look like a dork.

"Malt Vinegar, want some?"

He's offering the bottle and I can't imagine why you'd put vinegar on anything, but since he's English I figure he knows what he's doing when it comes to fish and chips so I grab the bottle and start sprinkling. When I take my first bite, I'm surprised that I like it.

"So," he says, covering his mouth while he chews and talks simultaneously, "I may have to go back across the pond sooner than I expected."

"What?" I nearly choke on a chip.

"Well, I'm not sure yet, but we have some contract issues that I might have to take care of back home."

"You mean, back in London?" Oh god, duh, of course he means London.

"Yeah, maybe as soon as next week."

He wipes his mouth and takes a sip of his beer, then rakes his hand through his Hugh Grant hair and looks at me. "You see, we signed this band about six months ago and . . ."

And he's off, going on and on about business. I'm kind of listening, don't get me wrong, and I'm definitely trying to act interested and happy for him, but the last thing I want to talk about is his leaving. Shit! I mean, where does that leave me? Not to mention the plans that I've made with him that he doesn't know about yet. It's like everybody has somewhere to go, and I'm the only one without a plan. M's going to Princeton, Blake's going to New York, and Connor has the record company and London. It's like everyone has a map and a destination and I'm just wandering way off the trail.

Thinking about this stuff just makes it really clear that tonight is just tonight, it's completely temporary. A moment ago I was feeling so happy; just being in this cool place that was featured in a magazine, with an awesome guy that's a younger, cuter, version of Richard Branson, it felt like enough. But by tomorrow morning my crappy life will still be there, patiently waiting for me. This whole night is starting to feel as borrowed as the dress I'm wearing.

Connor looks at me with concern and says, "I'm sorry, am I boring you?"

"No, of course not," I say. I give him a smile and mask my thoughts, and when he reaches across the table to squeeze my hand, I squeeze back even harder.

Chapter 16

We're driving down Sunset looking for this club, and I'm thinking with the amount of time M and I spend down here, you'd think I would know where it is. But with Connor, it's a whole new scene.

So his hand is on my knee and it feels warm and nice, so I place my hand on top of his and notice how small mine is in comparison. I've made a pact with myself to not think about how he's leaving for London soon because I'm sure he goes back and forth a lot on business, which means he'll definitely be back. And then the next time I'll probably be going with him and my life will really start.

"It should be coming up on the right. Give a shout if you see it," he says.

"What's the name of it again?" I ask, fingering the hem of my dress and squinting out the window.

"B Bar."

"I think you just missed it." I look in my side-view mirror, watching the neon sign shrink as we drive past it.

"No worries," Connor says, and I clutch the edge of my seat as he makes an illegal U-turn and pulls into the tiny parking lot.

He's holding my hand when we walk inside, and I'm praying

that I won't get carded. But like Harry's, he knows everyone so it's not even an issue.

We sit at a small table near the stage, and Connor leans in and goes, "So the band I want to see is the opening act. I just need to hear a few songs then we can leave if you want. I don't know if you'll like them, they're a little mainstream, and personally I'd rather listen to blues, but there's just more money to be made in pop." He shrugs and smiles and I'm wondering if that's what Richard Branson thought when he signed the Sex Pistols.

So right when they dim the lights and some guy walks on stage to do a mike check, that Sam chick walks right up to our table, leans down, and gives Connor a shot of some major cleavage along with a transatlantic kiss, you know, like one on each cheek. I just sit there and watch them and my stomach feels weird and I'm not sure what to do. When she finally looks at me, I smile and say, "Hey."

"Hey," she says, but I can tell she doesn't mean it.

Connor looks at her then and says, "You remember Alex?"

And Sam just squints at me briefly then looks at Connor and says, "Not really. Should I?"

I just sit there and I don't say anything, even though I can think of like, a million snotty answers to that.

Then Connor goes, "Trevor's party?"

But Sam just gives this innocent shrug, like she's so sorry but she just meets too many important people to remember someone like me, then she grabs the chair next to Connor's and slides it just slightly too close to his. She looks over at me then and gives me a big fake smile and even though I don't smile back, I've got to admit, I'm feeling like I'm in a little over my head right now.

I watch her turn to Connor and start talking in a voice so low it's hard for me to hear, so I just sit there awkwardly and sip my water because I feel like I should do something but I don't really know what.

When the band comes on she finally stops talking and Connor reaches for my hand and gives me a kiss on the side of my neck. I can totally feel her watching us but when I look at her she just looks away.

He's right about the band. I mean, they're not all choreographed and bland in that Backstreet Boys kind of way, but they're definitely too top-ten list for me. But the lead singer is cute enough for MTV and that usually guarantees major record sales and *People* magazine covers.

Halfway through the fourth song Connor puts his mouth to my ear and whispers, "Wanna go?"

I turn and kiss him in a way that means yes and I hope that Sam is watching.

When we stand up to leave he says, "Sam we're taking off, I'll see you at the office tomorrow."

She looks surprised and says, "Where are you guys going? Maybe I'll join you."

Connor shakes his head and says, "We're going home. Calling it a night." Then he grabs my hand and pulls me away from the table and when I look back she's still watching us and it makes me feel really uncomfortable.

When we get to Connor's house I tell him I have to use the bathroom. Then like the second after he shows me where it is, I lock the door, turn on the faucet (so it will muffle the noise), then I practically ransack the place. I mean, I'm going at it like a jealous wife. Looking in his mirrored cabinet, his trash can, behind the plastic shower curtain, under the rug. I even look in the toilet tank because I saw that once on an old *Law and Order* episode.

And the truth is, I don't even know what the hell it is I'm looking for, but I just can't stop. I mean, maybe there will be a stray tube of lipstick lying around, something a blonde would wear. But I don't find anything, so then of course I feel totally ashamed.

I guess I could have saved myself the trouble of making this mess and then having to clean it up, by just coming right out and asking Connor what their deal is. But the truth is, he's not my boyfriend (yet), so it's really none of my business (so far).

Connor is in the living room sitting on the couch in front of a gas log fire. The room is all white walls with no art, no plants, just an overstuffed couch and an old carved door propped up on cinder blocks, and now serving as a coffee table covered in piles of papers, magazines, and CDs. There's some great-sounding blues coming from the speakers and I stand in front of him and ask, "Who is this?"

"Jonny Lang." He grabs my hand and pulls me down next to him.

"He's really good, who is he?" I take a sip from the glass of red wine he hands me and try to calm my nerves.

"He's just a kid. Well, actually he's maybe twenty now, but he was only seventeen when he made this. That's him on guitar and vocals."

I sit on Connor's couch and listen to the sound of yet another teenage overachiever, fully aware of Connor referring to a seventeen year old as "just a kid."

When he puts his arm around me and kisses me, I banish all thoughts of Sam, my crazy jealousy, and Jonny Lang's age, and just try to live in the now.

So, we're on the couch making out and, well, I'll spare some of the details, even though that's the stuff people usually want to know about. Anyway, he unzips my dress and pulls it all the way off and tosses it on the floor. I'm lying there, naked except for my new thong, but now he's pulling that off too, and even though he didn't compliment me on my choice of underwear I'm still glad I bought it because cotton panties would have been embarrassing.

He kisses me everywhere and I even let him continue where we left off last time in the cabana. It's nice, but I'm not sure how long I'm supposed to lie there like that, so I push him off, and start helping him undress. And when we're both lying naked on this beige, slip-covered couch I slide down and do to him what he just did to me. I don't know if that's too gross to mention, but the fact is, I know how to give a blow job. Anyone who remains a virgin as long as I have pretty much has that covered.

So then he pulls me back up so we're face to face and then he reaches his hand down to the ground and fumbles around until he finds his jeans. His weight is sort of shifting on me and it's kind of getting uncomfortable but when he comes back up with a condom I breathe a sigh of relief since I really didn't know how to bring that up. Then all of a sudden he's inside me and we're doing it. And then we do it again. And then we go into his bedroom and fall asleep. And it didn't hurt, and I didn't bleed, so go figure.

Chapter 17

When I wake up the next morning, Connor has his arms wrapped tightly around me and I can feel his warm breath on the back of my neck, and I close my eyes and think about how glad I am that I held out so that he was my first. Because I've never, in my entire life, felt as happy, warm, and safe as I do right now. I finally know what it feels like to be in love.

Then he whispers in my ear, "Are you awake?"

And when I nod my head yes, he moves on top of me, and I just lay there kind of still because I'm still not exactly sure just how much I'm supposed to move around. And it's not long until he grips me tightly, and mumbles my name, then he kisses me all over my face (but not on the mouth since neither one of us has brushed our teeth yet), then he rolls off me and says, "I'll be right back."

I lay on my side watching his butt as he walks across the room, and I think about what M said, how losing your virginity is no big deal. But I totally disagree because it really kind of is. I mean, even though I'm still the same person, my relationship with Connor is totally different now. I just feel so much closer to him.

I roll over and look at the clock next to the bed and totally panic when I see that it's already seven-thirty. Shit! There's just no way I'm gonna be able to shower and make it to school in time for first period.

I jump out of bed and run into the living room and start frantically gathering all my clothes together. As I'm struggling with my shoes Connor walks into the room and goes, "What are you doing?"

"Getting dressed," I say as I balance on one heel and adjust the strap.

"Why?" He rubs his eyes, and squints at me.

"Because I'm late."

"Late for what?" He comes over and kisses me. "Come on, take the morning off, we'll have breakfast."

I lean my body into his for a moment and he feels so nice and warm, but then I push him away and get down on my knees and look under the old door/coffee table for my purse. "I can't," I tell him as I reach around on the floor. "I ditched school yesterday and I'm in enough trouble already."

Then I stand up and brush the creases out of my dress and when I look at him I realize I just outed myself. I stand there frozen, holding my stupid kitty purse, knowing that I can't undo this.

"Alex? What did you say?"

Connor is looking at me with a face full of suspicion, and I know I have to come clean so I take a deep breath and say, "Okay. Okay. I know you thought I was in college, but I'm not. I'm only seventeen, well, seventeen and a half actually, almost eighteen! And I'm a senior in high school." I gulp for air like an asthmatic.

Silence.

I take a step toward him and reach for his hand. It lacks emotion and lies limp in mine. "I'm sorry I lied. I guess I just figured you wouldn't want to hang out with me if you knew the truth. But, I'm still the same person, really! That's the only lie, I swear." I look at him desperately and continue to squeeze his nonresponsive fingers.

He's staring at me, and he doesn't look very happy. He shakes his head walks over to the couch, sits down and goes, "Listen, maybe you're right, maybe I wouldn't be hanging out with you if you'd told me you were still in high school. Shit! I'm twenty-three! I'm six years older than you!"

"Five and a half!"

"Alex, please. This is crazy! High school! God, I hesitated when you told me you were nineteen. And we had sex! And you're underage!" He looks really upset and it's all my fault.

"Well, it's not like I'm gonna call the cops! I mean, look, I'm sorry, really, I am." I sit next to him on the couch and try to control my panic.

Then he sighs and says, "Listen, the point is, you do seem a little young sometimes, but it never occurred to me that you were that young."

"I'm sorry," I say. It's all I can say.

I'm facing Connor but he won't look at me, he just sits there staring at the wall. After awhile he turns and says, "Look. You're nice and I've enjoyed hanging out with you. But I don't know about this. This is a little weird."

So then I get up from the couch and rifle through my purse for my keys and by the time I look up I've got my emotions under control just enough to say good-bye.

I'm walking toward the door, when I remember. My car is still parked on the street at Harry's and I don't know how I'm going to get it. I turn and look at Connor still sitting on the couch, but he's so unhappy with me, that I just can't ask him. So I say, "I'm sorry. I'm sorry that I disappointed you, I'm sorry I lied. But I had a nice time last night. Thank you."

I wait for him to say something more but he doesn't.

Chapter 18

I walk hurriedly to the corner and pull my cardigan tight around me. The morning is cold and bright and I wish I had my sunglasses with me, partly because of the sun and partly because my eyes and my dress look like last night and it's kind of embarrassing to be walking around like this.

When I get to the corner I stop and fish my wallet out of my purse to see how much cash I have left. I count only seven dollars and eighty-seven cents, since I spent most of it at the makeup counter and the lingerie department and you see what a good investment in my future that turned out to be.

I have no idea what to do, or how the hell I'm supposed to get to Century City from wherever it is I am. I mean, *I don't even know where I am!* All I know is that it's kind of far because I remember being in the car for awhile on the drive from Harry's and then B Bar. So I just sit on the curb and I put my head in my hands and try to suppress the panic that is building inside me. And I wonder if my life will ever stabilize. It's like at seven-fifteen Connor and I were making love and it felt like we were in love, and then just half an hour later I am *literally* on the curb.

I blow my nose into a slightly used tissue I find in my purse, then I crumble it up and stick it back in there. I'm sorry, if that's gross, but I'm totally opposed to littering. And then I grab my cell phone and call M.

"Hello?"

"M, it's me."

"Hey, where are you? What happened to you yesterday?"

"I'm in LA," I tell her.

"Are you with Connor?" she asks.

"Um, no. Listen, I'm kind of stuck and I need to get my car; it's parked in Century City. Can you come get me?"

"What? Are you kidding? First period starts in like three seconds," she says.

"I know, but I just thought," I bite down on my lower lip. I shouldn't have called her. God, I'm such a loser.

"I'm sorry, but I already missed Monday, I can't skip out today. But you know what you should do? You should call Connor, he'll totally help you," she says.

"Um, yeah, okay," I say, knowing there's no way I'm doing that, but I'm just not ready to tell her yet.

"See you in a few?"

"Yeah, definitely," I say, hanging up and wondering what to do next.

I stand up and brush the wrinkles out of my dress and head for this coffee shop that's just up the block. It looks pretty busy and I figure there's gotta be someone in there that can give me a little direction, or at least tell me where I am.

The place is packed with people who look like they spend most of their days sitting at a desk, in a cubicle, under bad fluorescent lighting. I mean, no one looks very friendly or helpful, so I just grab a place in line and hope that someone behind the counter can help me. When it's my turn I go, "Can you tell me what city this is?"

The girl behind the register just gives me this lousy look and says, "What? You don't know where you are?" Then she starts looking around like she's gonna call for backup or something.

"No, no," I say quickly. "No, of course I know where I am.

What I meant was can you tell me how to get to Century City from here?"

She drums her fingers on the register and goes, "Are you driving?"

"No, um, my car's there. I need to go get it."

"So why don't you take a cab or something?"

"Oh, okay," I say. "Do you know how much that will cost?"

"I don't know," she shrugs. "Ten, fifteen dollars?"

"Oh, that much?" I clutch my purse tighter, knowing that my wallet's close to empty.

She just looks at me, and I can tell she's quickly losing her patience.

"Um, do you have the number for a cab company?" I ask.

"Yeah, four-one-one. Listen, are you gonna get a coffee or what?" She shakes her head and rolls her eyes, and I can feel the people behind me getting impatient so I look at the board and search for the cheapest thing I can order, something that won't cut into my budget. And I go, "Yeah, um, I'll have a cup of the daily brew, oh, a small one please."

I hand over a dollar fifty and she gives me fifteen cents worth of coffee in return and I take it over to a crowded bar with a vacant seat. I put my purse on the counter in front of me and take a sip. It's way too hot, so I blow on it before I take the next one.

The guy on my right has a bad tie, razor burn, and a serious case of male pattern baldness. He's reading the *Wall Street Journal* and I'm guessing he won't want to help me. So I decide to ask the lady on my left, even though she looks only slightly friendlier.

"Hi," I say, interrupting her staring session with the wall. "Um, I was wondering if you could tell me how to get to Century City."

She looks at me and her eyes are etched with deep crow's feet and her nose is covered in these tiny red veins that look like they're exploding, and she doesn't seem as kind as I hoped she might be. "I don't know," she says. "Why don't you call a cab?"

"It's too expensive. I'm running out of money," I tell her.

She looks me over carefully then says, "Why don't you take the bus then? There's a stop on the next block. Why don't you go read the sign?"

I look at her and say, "Okay, thanks." But she doesn't hear me since she's already back to looking at the wall.

I look at my watch and it's eight-fifteen and I can't believe that my day already sucks this much. I mean, I have no idea how to take the bus. The only bus I've ever been on is the school bus. I consider walking back to Connor's and asking him for a ride to my car, but I can't do that. He's just not an option anymore. So I grab my coffee and my purse and head for the bus stop.

The driver is this old guy with a really stern face and I'm kind of afraid to talk to him so I let everyone go ahead and when there's no one left but me he goes, "If you want a ride you better get on now." I climb the two steps and reach for something to grab on to as he pulls away from the curb.

"Um, I was wondering if you could help me?" I ask.

He glances at me briefly and says, "Get behind the white line."

I look down at the floor and sure enough there's a line and I'm apparently on the wrong side of it. So I take a step back and now that I'm standing in the right spot I wonder if I should continue. He seems kind of mean.

He stops at the next light and turns and looks at me, and still stern but a little friendlier, he says, "What do you need?"

"I need to get to Century City and I'm not even sure if this is the right bus."

"This is the right bus," he says, changing gears with the changing light. "But it's only one of them."

"What?" I ask. I feel like we're speaking different languages. Like bus riding is a culture that I'm not a part of.

He shakes his head and goes, "You need to stay on this bus to Santa Monica Boulevard. From there you need to catch the number four to Century Park East. And from there you need to take the twenty-eight to Olympic."

He turns and looks at me and I'm just staring at him. I'll never remember all that. "But that's three different buses!" I say. "How much is that going to cost me?"

"A dollar twenty-five."

"Each?" I ask. Frantically doing the math in my head and hoping I'll have enough.

"Total. It's seventy-five cents plus twenty-five cents for each transfer."

"Where do I get those?" I ask. Digging through my wallet for change.

"You get one from me, and the other on the next bus," he says, handing me a strip of paper. "Now take a seat."

He brakes at the next stop and the bus lurches forward and back and I grab the first available seat because I'm lousy at keeping my balance in a moving vehicle. Then I just sit there and stare out the window at a string of run-down minimalls and try to remember the exact moment when I decided to give up.

By the time I'm at my third bus stop, I realize this is gonna take a lot longer than I thought and that the second-period bell rang a long time ago, and I never called my mom last night to tell her where I was. And even though all that stuff is true, I gotta tell you that part of me feels pretty damn good at having figured this out and getting this far on my own. I mean, most people would have just called a cab. But I didn't have that option so I took a more difficult route and made it all the same.

I dig my cell phone out of my purse and call my mom at work. She's away from her desk so I leave a message and say that I spent the night at M's, and I'm sorry I forgot to call, and that I'll see her tonight. Then I pray that she doesn't decide to follow up on any of that.

When I finally get to my car after a two-and-a-half-hour mass transit tour of LA, I find a piece of pink paper stuck under my windshield wiper. I reach for it excitedly, knowing it's from Connor, and I can't wait to read his apology. But when I turn it over I see that it's only a parking ticket, a love note from the LAPD. I fold it in half and toss it in my glove compartment and head to school.

Chapter 19

'm walking through the quad looking at my watch trying to figure out what class I should be heading to when M runs up and goes, "Is that my dress?"

I look down at the clothes I wore last night and just shrug and say, "Yeah, I guess it is."

"Are you okay?" she asks. " 'Cause you don't look so great."

"Thanks," I say and head for my locker.

"So, what happened?"

She's walking alongside me, giving me a concerned look. I think about the Iguana Man, and Connor dumping me, and the bus ride, and the fact that I'm still a little pissed at her for ditching me, but I just say, "I cut." Then I focus on spinning the lock, trying to remember my combination.

She doesn't say anything but I can hear the disapproval in her breath. Then she goes, "Remember when you told me how my mom was in my room Sunday night, you know, answering my phone and stuff?"

"Yeah." I close my locker and I start walking toward class. It's eleven o'clock, time for Economics, which I think I already had a real-life lesson in this morning.

"Well, shit, I think she found my stash."

"Your what?" I turn and look at her.

"My stash. You know some blunts and stuff that I had hidden in there."

I don't even know what to say to her. I can't believe she's doing drugs. I mean, sometimes I feel like I don't even know her.

"*Hello?* Did you hear me? Anyway, I'm kind of freakin' here. I don't know what to do."

"Are they your drugs?" I stop in the middle of the hall and stare at her.

"Yeah, it's all mine. And shit, I'm totally screwed."

"What kind of drugs did you have?" I ask.

"Shhh!" She looks around nervously then whispers, "Just pot and some X that Trevor and I were gonna do this weekend."

"Jeez, M, what are you doing with that stuff?"

"God, what is this? What are you, a cop?"

I don't say anything. I can't believe she's that far gone.

"Hel-lo?"

"Whatever." I start walking toward class.

"Okay, look. I told you, I'm freaking out."

"Well, what makes you think she found them?"

"Well, this morning I went to wear those JP Todd driving mocs? You know the ones I wear with my jeans and stuff? Well anyway, they're gone. I think my mom borrowed them. She booked herself in at some spa for the week and apparently she took those shoes with her, and unfortunately they're the ones I had my stash in."

"You hide your stash in your shoes?"

"I have immaculate feet."

"Why would you put it there? You know your mom's always taking your stuff."

"Because I didn't think she'd want to wear those. Shit!"

"Well, don't you think if she'd found it she'd cancel her plans and stay home to ask you about it?"

"My mom? Let a little parental responsibility get in the way of a massage and a Botox injection? I don't think so." She shakes her head.

"Well, when is she coming back?" I ask.

"Not until Sunday."

"So, at least you've got the rest of the week to figure a way out of it."

"Yeah, I guess. Hey, so did you call Connor?"

I open the classroom door. I'm not ready to talk about Connor. "M," I say, "you're gonna be late for your psych class. I'll see you at lunch okay?" She gives me a strange look but I close the door on her anyway.

So I buy a salad and a bottle of water and carry it over to our lunch tree, where M is waiting with M&Ms and a Diet Coke. She rips the bag open and starts separating them by color, then she hands me all of the brown ones and lies back on the grass. "Hey, do you have to work today after school?" she asks.

"Yeah, but I'm thinking about calling in sick." God, I'm just losing interest in everything these days.

"Good. Let's go to LA. But, by ourselves, let's not call the guys. Let's just do our own thing."

I'm just about to tell her that my day started in LA and that calling the guys is no longer an option for me, when Tiffany and Amber approach us. Tiffany's wearing a sparkly sling in our school colors and they're standing in front of us, and they look all happy to be hanging out together so I guess that whole Dylan/flirting/vomiting fiasco is over. They look at us and go, "Hey M, hey Alex."

We just look at them and go, "Hey."

Then Tiffany looks me over and goes, "Nice dress."

I say, "Thanks," but I wonder if that was actually sarcasm I heard in her voice.

"So who are you guys going to THE PROM with?" That's how she says it, in capital letters.

I look at her and go, "When is it?"

And now Amber looks at Tiffany and rolls her eyes and shakes her head and Tiffany says, "Hel-*lo*? It's like totally coming up. There's signs all over campus. You still go here right?"

Wow. That was pretty bitchy for someone who recently vomited orange right in front of me. But I just sit there in front of them and shrug and say, "Well, I guess I'm not going then."

"What? Why?" They're both scrutinizing me now, and I know they think I'm hiding something. That deep down inside I must be feeling really sad to not be taking part in this most sacred of high school rituals. They've spent the better half of senior year preparing for this, you know bagging the right date and buying the right dress. It's like almost as important as their SATs. I mean, it's sick how seriously they take all this stuff.

So then Tiffany goes, "Well don't you have a boyfriend or something? I thought I heard M say that you're dating someone."

I look over at M wondering why she would be talking about me to Tiffany but she just shrugs. Then I look back at Tiffany and Amber, standing there, judging me. And I hate to admit it, but part of me cares about what they think. Part of me wants to have something important. So I tell them all about Connor, even though he doesn't really exist for me anymore.

"Well," I say, "actually, I am dating someone. His name is Connor and he's from London, England, but he lives in Los Angeles right now and he owns his own record company. So if the prom is on a Saturday night, then we'll probably be at a club or something so we wont be able to make it." Then I sit back and watch them chew on *that*.

Amber looks at me and raises her eyebrows but doesn't say anything. And Tiffany nods her head and goes, "Cool." And I actually think I detect a little envy.

Then they look at M and ask her if she's going and M nods her head and goes, "Totally."

And I look at her waiting to hear more, but that's all the information she's giving.

And then Tiffany goes, "Well, we're working on the yearbook, as you know, and we're going to have a sort of 'Senior Inspiration' page in it."

I look at them and say, "You guys have been watching way too much *Oprah*."

M cracks up but they don't think it's funny. So then they go, "What we're doing is going around and asking certain seniors what their biggest achievement has been in their lives so far."

And I'm thinking "certain seniors" means just the popular people. Unpopular people are lucky just to get their class picture published. God, I totally hate this stuff.

So they're looking at M waiting for an answer and she's really deep in thought, obviously taking this question very seriously. Then she goes, "My biggest achievement thus far is being named in the *Who's Who Among American High School Students*."

I look at her in shock. I didn't even know there was such a thing. They write it down and then look at me waiting for my answer. But I just look at them and shrug and go, "Um, I guess my biggest achievement so far is growing my bangs out." They look at me to see if I'm joking, but I'm not. So they write it down and walk away and I'm thinking I can't wait to see that in print.

The bell rings; man I hate how lunch hour really isn't an hour. I pick up my trash and head to the class I dread the most, AP History. I know it's shallow, but I'm so stuck in the now that it's hard for me to care about things that happened, like, a hundred years ago.

Chapter 20

S o I'm sitting at my desk in AP History, and I'm surrounded by the same people from most of my other classes. All us AP people stick together, we just change rooms that's all. On my desk, lying face down is my test paper from last week. And I really don't want to flip it over because I already know that I choked, and I don't need to see it. I mean, I didn't even read the questions, I just made a perfect zigzag by shading in the *a, b, c, d,* and *e,* circles accordingly, and then I turned it in.

Everyone is eagerly flipping them over and shouting out their results, but I just sit there. I've got a major headache, I'm nauseous and I'm totally sweating. I mean, I'm a wreck. I feel like bolting out of class but I don't want to attract that kind of attention. I know that my life is really getting out of control, that I'm just totally blowing it for myself, but I just can't seem to stop it. I raise my hand and ask my teacher if I can get a hall pass for the restroom. He gives me the pass and a disapproving look.

I grab my test paper, and stash it in my purse and run out of the room. I barely make it to the stall when I start vomiting. The salad I just ate is history. I drag myself over to the mirror and stare intently at my reflection. I look like a girl who didn't go home last night. I look like a girl that normal girls back away from. I splash cold water on my face, swish it around in my mouth and spit it back into the sink. Then I brush my hair, and fix my makeup, and swallow a mint that I found unwrapped at the bottom of my purse.

I look better now, but I still feel awful and I know that it's not at all physical but completely emotional. I pull my test paper out of my purse, and rip it into tiny shreds. I drop the pieces slowly into the trash, watching them fall, but never once looking at my score. I'm not even curious.

I'm tempted to stay in the bathroom until the bell rings. I'm tempted to stay in here until graduation. But then this girl walks in, leans against the wall, gives me a sullen look, and lights a cigarette. We just sort of look at each other then she says, "Hey, what class are you ditching?"

"AP History," I say. "But I'm not ditching. I just had to use the bathroom."

She takes a drag on her cigarette. "AP? Really?" She squints at me through the smoke.

"Yeah really. Why?" I ask, somewhat defensively.

She shrugs, "I just didn't picture you as the type."

I just look at her for a moment and I wonder what she means by that. "What year are you?" I ask.

"Sophomore."

Well that explains it. She doesn't know my history. She didn't know me in my glory days. "I used to be involved," I tell her. "I used to win contests, and elections. I used to care about things. I wasn't always like this," I say.

"Whatever." She rolls her eyes and takes another drag.

And I'm left standing there feeling like a loser for going on like that. Because the truth is, it doesn't really matter who I used to be. It's all about who I've become.

"Well anyway," I say, turning to leave.

"Hey do you have a breath mint so I won't reek when I go to my next class?" she asks.

"No," I tell her, shaking my head. "You're on your own."

———

When I walk back in the classroom my teacher totally ignores me. I mean, his lecture doesn't miss a beat, and I'm wondering if I'm invisible to people now. Like I'm so pathetic that people just refuse to see me. I sit at my desk and realize I have no idea what this lecture is about, or even what we are supposed to be studying. A couple of students raise their hands to ask questions, and I am amazed at their powers of concentration. I wonder if they really care about the answers or if they've just figured out that he likes it when you show interest.

After thirty minutes of doodling on a piece of notebook paper, pretending I'm taking notes, the bell finally rings and I gather my things and get up to leave when my teacher asks me if I could stay a minute. I don't really want to but I realize it's what you call a rhetorical question. I slowly sink back into my chair and try to ignore the smirks of my fellow AP students as they leave the room. When the last one is gone, he gets up and shuts the door and takes a seat at the desk next to mine. I'm sweating big time and don't care for the proximity, but I remain silent, I mean, I just sit there.

"Are you aware that you're failing this class?" he says.

I nod.

"Well, I'm wondering what we are going to do about it."

I'm thinking, *"We?"* but I just shrug.

"I'm wondering why I can't seem to reach you." He leans toward me and it's creeping me out. "I take it somewhat personally when a bright student like you fails. It makes me feel as though I'm also failing, by not being able to reach you, by not being able to inspire you."

And then I get it. What he really wants is for me to confirm what a great teacher he is. For me to take full responsibility for my sorry performance. To let him off the hook. I'm more than willing to do this. If it means cutting this short, I'll say just about anything. So I clear my throat and say, "I've been having a rough year at home. I have to work. I mean, I'm working a lot, and sometimes I have trouble concentrating, but it's absolutely, entirely, one hundred percent my fault. You are a wonderful teacher, really inspiring, it's just me, it's all me, the problem is mine." This seems to satisfy him. Adults are no different from us. They're all ego and insecurity.

I bolt out of class, I mean, I really run. I don't stop until I get to the parking lot and see M waiting in her car. I jump in without opening the door, and M goes, "Wow, that's what Brandon used to do on *90210.*" I throw my books on the floor and crank the volume on her car stereo. I put on my sunglasses and sit back and decide to just let go of it all, to just be in the moment. To locate my Zen spot. Some students wave at us as we pull out of the parking lot, but we just totally ignore them. We get on the freeway and head to LA.

"Where should we go?" M asks.

That's kind of a weird question because we always just do the same old stuff. Veggie rolls, shopping, coffee, drinking, meeting people, then singing to some CD all the way home. I just look at her and shrug, "I don't know, the usual I guess." And then I go, "No, you know what? Let's do something different. I'm really up for something new, aren't you?" And I think I am. I mean, the last person I want to run into is the Iguana Man. Well, the Iguana Man and Connor.

Chapter 21

We decide to go to Griffith Park Observatory and check out the telescopes. I haven't been there since a class trip in sixth grade when we briefly studied the solar system, and all the planets and stuff, and I dreamed, (for a short time) about being an astronomer.

I had the biggest crush ever on the second cutest boy in the class. His name was Bobby and M had a crush on the first cutest boy in the class, Bobby's best friend Wes.

So that day we were all nervous about who we were going to sit with on the bus and who we were going to sit with in *the dark* during the laser show. I remember some notes being exchanged and some whispering going on for days beforehand and even though we didn't sit next to them on the bus, we definitely sat next to them during the show. And since it was dark and the teachers and chaperones were all in another row, Bobby reached over and held my hand. And at one point, while the laser lights were all dancing to that Rolling Stones song, "Angie," he kissed me on the lips. It was the kind of kiss we used to call a "romantic kiss," which meant it wasn't from a relative, it lasted more than ten seconds, and it involved two tongues. I remember feeling so great about it, and being so happy. And to this day I cannot listen to that song without thinking of Bobby holding my hand and kissing me.

We're driving up the long, winding road that leads to the Observatory when M blurts out, "My dad is having an affair." The statement just sort of hangs in the air, taking shape. And I'm really surprised, though I'm not sure why. I guess I just always thought M would be protected from all that.

Not knowing what else to say, I ask, "Are you sure?"

"Oh, yeah. I'm sure." She turns to look at me briefly. "I saw him with another woman. Remember that medical conference he was supposed to be at? Well he wasn't. He was in LA shacking up with his girlfriend at the Hotel Bel Air. Trevor and I went there for lunch on Sunday and I saw them at the bar. They were holding hands but they may as well have been fucking."

I just sit there, looking at her.

Then she shakes her head and says, "And do you know what the worst part is, the really fucking sick part? My mom knows. I know she knows. I can tell. She's known all along. And it's not like she's taking some liberal, European view of these things. Oh no. She just looks the other way because she's enjoying the cars, and vacations, and credit cards so damn much. Just can't bear to give all that up. She has no intention of going to work, or even setting a goddamn alarm clock for that matter. It's probably been going on for years. But she'd rather be well dressed and in denial, than grab hold of her life and not be two-timed like that. You should have seen them together, they looked really happy."

"Did he see you?" I ask.

She sighs, "No, and that's the good thing because I wasn't where I said I would be, but then again, neither was he."

"So what happens now? Do you think they'll get divorced?"

She looks in her rearview mirror and changes lanes. "Not a chance. My mom would never allow it, and my dad's got the best of both worlds, why would he mess with that? God, the least she could do is screw the pool boy, I might have more respect for her if she did that."

M says that, but I know she doesn't mean it.

"Do you realize how important it is to be independent? To be able to take care of yourself? To not rely on someone else for your most basic needs? And to not get so damn attached to stuff that you'd rather demean yourself than live without it?" She grips the steering wheel and looks at me and I tell her I'm pretty well versed in all of that.

She parks the car and we walk toward the building. Night is falling quickly and I run over to the nearest telescope, insert a quarter, and look at all the big houses until the sun disappears. Then we go inside and walk around reading the exhibits and looking at the people. There's a pretty big crowd here for the laser show, and they're not all stoners either.

M buys me a ticket and we grab two seats and wait for the show to start. I feel sorry for M, I really do. I've been where she is. I know what it's like to have your parents play Russian Roulette with your future.

The lights go out and I lay my head back on the padded neck rest. I watch the ceiling light up in a riot of color and sound as the squiggly stars and lights dance to seventies glam rock, David Bowie, Lou Reed, Iggy Pop. I love all that old music. I look over at M and see that she's crying so I look away, giving her some privacy.

Chapter 22

After the show we end up at this little sushi joint that unfortunately is not far from Connor's house. And I'm sitting here feeling really nervous, and wishing I was somewhere else, because I don't want to see him. But I couldn't tell M that, because she's so upset about her dad, and she really wanted sushi, and it's almost like if I don't talk about it, then I can pretend it didn't really happen. Which is probably a sign of mental instability, but I can't help it, I'm just not ready to face it.

M orders two big hot sakes and nearly one of everything on the menu. But I just stick with the California rolls. I like my fish cooked. I'm making a humiliating attempt to eat with my chopsticks when she goes, "So what really happened to you yesterday and this morning?"

I look at her and I know I should tell the truth, that my lying is really getting out of control, but I don't want to talk about the bad stuff so I go, "I hung out with Connor." Then I look down at my plate, determined to secure my California roll between those stupid chopsticks.

"Really?" she asks.

"Really," I tell her. Then I plop the roll into my mouth and when I'm done chewing I go, "And we slept together."

"No way!"

"Way." I look at her and nod my head affirmatively.

"And? Come on, you have to tell me," she pleads.

"And . . . it was . . . good," I say, suddenly wishing I hadn't mentioned it.

But she nods her head eagerly, waiting for something more, so I lean in and go, "We did it like, three times."

"Really?" she says.

Her eyes are wide and she's looking right at me, and I hate to lie but so far, technically, everything I said is true. "Really . . . it was really . . . nice," I say.

"Wow. Are you guys like, in love now?"

I look down at my plate and shrug.

"Come on, give it up. I can tell you're totally into him."

I just shrug, and when I look at her I try to smile but it feels false on my face.

"You know Alex, I can't believe how lucky we are right now. I mean, I have Trevor, you have Connor, and it's like, so big time, you know?"

"Yeah," I say, and then I look over at the door and freeze.

M sees me looking and goes, "Oh my god! Isn't that Connor?"

I look down at my plate because I don't want him to see me looking at him. "Who's he with?" I whisper.

She squints toward the door. "Some strange-looking guy I don't know and some blond chick."

"Does she look like Madonna?" I hold my breath.

"No, more like Heather Graham."

"That's what I mean," I say. "Ray of Light Madonna." And then I look up again, just in time to see Connor, James, and that girl Sam leaving the restaurant.

"They're leaving! Aren't you gonna say hi?" M looks at me in disbelief.

"No." I shake my head, but my eyes are glued to the door.

"You're such a chicken!"

She starts to get up from the table to do it for me, when I go, "M, no!"

But she ignores me and stands up and goes, "Connor! Hey!"

And while she's waving her arms around, I'm sinking lower in my chair. I see Sam look back at me and roll her eyes. But James doesn't see me because he's already out the door. Then Connor stops and turns and looks right at me and I feel my stomach go all weird, and I'm hoping that he'll smile and come over and tell me he's sorry, and he misses me, and he wants me back. But instead he just hesitates at the door, gives me a sort of half wave, and then follows his friends outside.

M stares after him and goes, "What was that about? Why did he leave?"

I just shake my head and go, "There's something I didn't tell you." And I feel like a total loser for having to say what I'm about to.

And then I tell her everything.

When I'm finished she just looks at me and goes, "You kept this in all day? Until now?"

I nod.

"Why? Why didn't you tell me?"

"I couldn't." I look down at my chopsticks and tap them against the side of my plate.

"Oh man. I don't even know what to say."

"Well that's a first." I try to laugh but it feels like the end of the world.

"God, I'm so sorry. Connor's a jerk. I can't believe he just walked out like that, without saying anything. What an ass."

I shake my head. "No, he's not. He's just a guy. And I lied to him." I bite down on my lower lip and try to keep from crying.

"Oh my god, do you think he's doing it with that Sam chick?" M asks, her eyes wide.

"I can't even think about that," I say.

She looks at me for a long time then she goes, "I'm really sorry."

I just shrug.

"Well, at least you're not a virgin anymore."

"What's that supposed to mean?" I ask.

"Well, it's just that it's out of the way now. You can just move on. It's like, now it won't be such a big deal to you."

I run my finger along the rim of my empty sake cup and say, "Well, I don't know about that. I mean, it kind of is a big deal and I can't imagine it ever not being a big deal." I shake my head. "Do you remember that time we got really tanked on vodka, and watched your dad's porno tapes?"

M starts laughing, "Yeah, we were sophomores, right?"

"Yeah. Well, when we were watching those, I remember thinking that there was no way that all that suntanned, silicone, video stuff really represented the real thing. I just couldn't believe it could be that detached when you let some other person inside your body. Do you remember how in that one movie, the star, right in the middle of some heavy thrusting, checked out the time on her watch?"

M laughs. "Yeah, I guess they missed that in the editing room."

"Well, when I first woke up I felt so happy and special. You know, like I had something really good in my life. But later, when it was over and I was out on the street, I felt like the girl with the watch. I felt disposable."

"Don't say that." M looks at me, alarmed.

"It's true. That's how I feel. And I'll probably never see him again, since it's pretty clear he doesn't want to see me." I push my sake cup away and fold my napkin.

M looks at me and grabs my hand from across the table. "You know what?" she says. "Most of the time it doesn't work out. That's just the way it is."

Then she pays the bill with her dad's credit card and we go home.

Chapter 23

When I walked in the door I found my mom sitting at the kitchen table, apparently waiting up for me. Something about the look on her face told me I was in big trouble.

"Alexandra, where have you been?" she asks.

Okay, she hasn't done this to me, like, ever. And it's making me nervous but I just go, "At school, and then I went shopping with M."

"And yesterday?"

And I go, "Yeah, and yesterday too." Because it's not really a lie if you think about it. I mean, I did start my day at school and I did go shopping.

"That's not what the school says."

"What do you mean?" I nervously shift my purse to my other shoulder and wait.

"They called me at work to say that you had an unexcused absence yesterday, and that you missed your first three classes this morning. They say you weren't there, you say you were. Who's right?"

She's not fooling around and I know I can't lie anymore. I mean, all these lies are just making everything worse. So I take a deep breath and go, "Um, they are?"

She nods her head and drums her fingers on the table. After a moment she asks, "And where were you if you weren't at school?"

I rub the toe of my shoe against the linoleum floor and say, "With a friend." And I feel like the world's biggest loser.

"Which friend? M?"

I take a deep breath, "No."

My mom just looks at me and shakes her head and says, "I don't know what to do with you anymore. But you cannot go on like this. Not under my roof. You've completely abused the freedom I gave you so now I'm going to take it away. You're grounded."

"What?"

"Until further notice."

"You can't ground me!" I say.

"I just did. I want you in school every day, and on the nights you're not working I want you home doing your homework."

"Like it matters," I mumble under my breath and start to leave the room.

"What did you say to me?"

"I said, what does it matter?" I turn around and face her and I'm screaming but I don't care. "I told you the truth, but you punish me anyway! It's like I can't win no matter what I do!"

"Has it ever occurred to you that maybe you won't let yourself win?"

I stand in front of her and roll my eyes, but I don't say anything.

"Alex, you have to apply yourself to something! You cannot continue like this."

"In case you don't get it mom, I'm not going to college! I messed up my grades so bad that I can't get a scholarship, and Dad won't help me because he sunk all of his money into his midlife-crisis kit with his bachelor pad, his Porsche, and his girlfriend's new boobs! And you certainly can't help me. So why bother with high school? Why try?"

My mom just looks at me and shakes her head and says, "Because at seventeen your mistakes are not permanent. There's no reason you can't turn your life around." She looks more frustrated than mad.

"Whatever," I roll my eyes and shake my head.

"You are the only one who can make your dreams happen." She says it quietly and emphatically and it really pisses me off.

"What're you quoting Hallmark now?" I give her an angry look.

"I'm serious. If you want to make something of yourself, it's going to be up to you. Don't expect other people to help you."

"Nobody gets it," I scream.

"Maybe you're the one that doesn't get it." She gives me a hard look and I grab my stuff and I run out of the kitchen. And when I get to my room I slam the door as hard as I can and throw my stuff against the wall and watch it fall to the ground. Then I pick up that stupid *Anna K* book and rip the cover off and crumple it up and toss it in the trash. Then I throw myself on my bed, and wonder if this is what "rock bottom" feels like.

Chapter 24

The next day at school I'm walking to our lunch tree and I can't help but notice all the sparkly prom signs hanging all over campus. It's like Tiffany and her prom crew went a little crazy with the silver glitter, and exclamation points. Apparently this year's theme is "My Heart Will Go On" and since I'm trying to be more honest I'm just gonna come right out and say how much I despise that song, and don't even get me started on the person who sings it.

Yet part of me also feels bad about not being able to care about this stuff. It's like the whole damn school is so into this. I mean, the girls that aren't going think about it just as much as the girls that are going. And I wish I could be on either one of those teams. Either the excited ones that're busy buying their stupid celebrity-knock-off prom dresses, or the reject ones who will sit in their rooms on prom night listening to that stupid prom song over and over again and wishing they were important, and popular like Tiffany, or Amber, or maybe even M. And I wish this because if I belonged to either one of these groups that would mean that I care about something that matters to other people. That would make me someone who belongs to something. But like this, I'm totally on my own. I mean, if what they say is true, if these are truly the best years of my life, then I'm totally screwed.

M is waiting for me under the tree, with a big fruit salad her maid packed for her this morning, and just as I figured, she's totally panicked about snagging a prom date. And there's no way she's asking Trevor. I mean, she might kind of like showing him off, but she's also pretty hesitant about involving him in the more juvenile side of her life. So now she's in a total state of emergency since she pretty much spent the better part of our junior and senior years blowing off every guy in our school that had the slightest interest in her. So now she's gonna have to find someone from another school. Only she doesn't really know anyone from any other school.

"Shit, what am I gonna do?" she asks.

"I thought you didn't care about going to the prom?" I say, stealing a strawberry.

She looks at me and rolls her eyes and goes, "You know I have to go. I'm a cheerleader for god's sake, how will it look if I don't show up?"

"And what will you tell your grandchildren?" I reach for a piece of pineapple.

The warning bell rings but we just continue to sit there. "So what's going on this weekend?" she asks. "Are we hanging in LA or what?"

"Maybe you are but, technically, I'm grounded," I tell her.

"What?"

"You heard me."

"I heard you but I can't believe what I heard. Aren't we a little too old for that?"

"That's what I thought, but my mom has other ideas." I take another strawberry and hand her the lid to the plastic container.

"You're not going along with it are you?" M looks at me like I'm crazy.

"Well, actually, I'm thinking that if I'm good today and tomorrow then maybe I'll get time off for good behavior this weekend."

"That's just weird," M shakes her head.

"Tell me."

"Have you heard from Connor?"

"No. Thanks for asking though." I shake my head.

"I didn't mean anything by it. I'm kind of surprised really. You know he told Trevor that we were underage."

"And?"

"Trevor didn't seem to care, he thought it was kind of funny. He likes the idea of corrupting a minor. Pervert."

I just roll my eyes. "Hey, did anything ever come of that missing stash?"

M starts gathering her things and stands up. "Yeah, my mom found it when she went to wear those shoes," she says without looking at me.

"And you didn't mention that until just now? What happened?"

M just shrugs, "It's really no big deal. I'm not in trouble if that's what you're worried about."

"You mean she didn't care?" I ask.

"Well, we talked about it last night on the phone, but I convinced her that I don't have a problem and they're not mine."

I notice that she still won't look at me. "What? Did you blame it on the maid?" I stand there staring at her; she's acting really strange.

She starts walking away, then turns around and says, "No, I just said I was holding it for someone. Listen, I need to get to class. You do too. We'll talk later okay?"

I just stand there and watch her walk away and wonder what is going on with her.

Chapter 25

S o, my mom did not give me the weekend off for good behavior. Apparently she is taking this whole discipline thing
very seriously. And even though I think it's a little late in
the game to start all this, the pathetic truth is that other
than going to work, I don't have anything else to do anyway.

So Sunday morning I'm sitting at my desk, working on my Tolstoy paper, if you can believe it. I even woke up early to get started
on it since I spent last night in front of the TV, and everyone knows
that Saturday night network TV is nothing but bad sitcoms, and
bad made-for-TV movies starring former stars of bad sitcoms. I
mean, you can just picture those overpaid network executives sitting around some big table, drinking mineral water and saying
things like, "Just put on any old piece of shit from seven to midnight since only losers watch on the weekends."

Well, my mom knocks on my door, and when I get up to open
it she's standing there with a strange look on her face. Then she
says, "M's here."

I open the door wide and find M standing behind my mom
and now I know what the weird look was all about. I pull M into
my room and quickly close the door on my mom's curiosity.

I watch her plop herself onto my bed and I go, "So what's

going on with you? You look, tired," I say. Even though everyone knows that "tired" really means "awful."

"Thanks a lot," she says rolling her eyes. "Do you have something I can change into?"

I open a drawer and toss her a pair of sweatpants and a tank top. She strips off a tiny black dress I've never seen before and a pair of Jimmy Choo sandals that belong to her mother, puts on the sweats, then grabs a tissue from a box on my dresser and starts wiping off last night's makeup.

"So you want to hear it?" She looks at me through the mirror.

"Whenever you're ready," I tell her.

"Okay." She sits on my bed with one eye still made up and goes, "Trevor and I had a little argument this morning. We broke up."

"Oh my god, what happened?" I ask.

She gets up from the bed and walks toward the mirror. She stands in front of it looking at herself and then grabs a tissue and goes to work on the other eye. "You won't even believe it," she says.

"Tell me."

"Start to finish? Or just the good stuff?"

"Whatever."

"Okay, well, we were out last night having fun at this club, hanging out in the VIP room, which by the way, is so awesome, I don't know if I can ever not be in a VIP room. Anyway, Trevor goes to the bathroom and some friend of his asks me if I want to dance. So I'm like, 'Okay,' so we start dancing. Then Trevor comes back and when he sees me he comes over and taps me on the shoulder and says he wants to go home."

"Why did he want to go home?"

"'Cause he's an ass that's why." She's finished with her eye and now she's using my hairbrush. "So anyway, I'm having a good time and I really don't feel like leaving, but I'm not gonna argue about it either, so I wave good-bye to his friend and follow Trevor outside. So we're in the car driving home and he asks me if I had a good time dancing with Jake. So I go, 'Who's Jake?' And he goes, 'Jake is the guy you were dancing with.' And I go, 'I'm a little lost here, where are you going with this?' And he goes, 'I'm going nowhere, we're going nowhere.' And I go, 'Whatever.'"

"What was that all about?" I ask. "That doesn't sound like Trevor."

"It sounds like all of them if you think about it, competitive, territorial, caveman! So then we get back to the house and do a little X."

"You did ecstasy?"

She rolls her eyes.

"Jeez, I still can't believe you're doing X."

"Don't get all preachy on me. It's practically easier to do X than to not do X these days. You're like some, I don't know, DEA wannabe." She makes a face at me and pulls her long blonde hair back into a ponytail.

"Whatever." I grab a magazine and start flipping through it.

"Okay, I'm sorry. Listen, I just wanted to try it. I mean, what's the big deal? It just makes you feel really really happy. *You* should try it."

"I'm already really, really happy," I tell her.

"Alex, I don't want to argue with you. I've had a long night."

I roll my eyes.

"Okay, so where was I? Oh yeah, we take the pills and we crank some music and get a little wild. You know, just running around, dancing and stuff. At some point we pass out. Then when we wake up this morning we're rolling around under the sheets when my hand gets caught in something. So I pull my hand out from under the blanket to see what it is and hanging off of my wrist is a pair of little, pink, thong panties. I hold my hand up to the light and just look at them for a minute. Then I put my hand right up in Trevor's face, really close you know, and I say, 'You bastard!' He looks like a deer caught in headlights and he's trying to say that they're mine."

"But you hate pink," I say.

"Exactly. So then I go, 'You fucking bastard! You didn't even change the fucking sheets!' Then I throw the panties at him and they land on his head!" She starts laughing then. "You should have seen it. He looked like that picture of Monica Lewinsky that they always show! You know the one where she's wearing the beret? So then I get up, grab my clothes, and go into the bathroom. Asshole is banging on the door all the while trying to get me to come out. He's got a really good explanation he says. And all I can think of is last night when he blasts me for very innocently dancing with Jake, or whatever his name is. That is sooo typical. It's always the guilty one who convicts!" She uses what's left of my Dior Addict sample, dabbing it on each wrist, and lies down on my bed.

"When I finally vacate the bathroom I find him sleeping in the hall next to the door. So just as I'm trying to step over him he grabs my ankle and begs me to just please listen to him. I tell him to let go of my ankle. And he goes, 'Just please listen to me,' and I go, 'Let go of my ankle or I'm gonna kick you.' And he goes, 'C'mon M.' And then I kick him and I go, 'See I told you I was gonna kick you. I'm not the liar here.' And then I left." She looks at me and shakes her head.

"Wow."

"Tell me about it."

"All of that happened last night?" I ask.

"Can you believe it?" She sits up and reaches in her purse for a cigarette.

"Don't smoke that, my mom will freak."

"Oh, sorry." I watch her toss it back in her purse.

"So whose panties were they?"

"I don't care." She shrugs.

"Are you sure? Because it kind of seems like you do."

"What am I supposed to do? Take them in for DNA testing?"

I just shrug. "So what are you gonna do?"

"Ignore him and act like I don't care."

"So you do care."

"Of course I care! We were having such a good time together! My god, first my dad, and now Trevor. Chain of pain, it never ends."

"I'm sorry."

"Yeah, me too. Hey, I'm really tired," she says. "Do you mind if I sleep here for a little while? I don't feel like going home."

"Why? Are your parents there?" I ask.

She shakes her head. "No, I've barely seen them all month. I just don't feel like being alone right now."

"Feel free," I say.

She lies down and pulls the comforter up over her head and dozes off immediately. I sit in my chair and watch her sleep and think how weird it is that she doesn't want to go home. I always thought M was really lucky that her parents were never around. I mean, she just has so much freedom. I guess I never realized that she might not see it as such a great thing.

It's weird because M's parents are still married but it's like she's divorced from them, and my parents are divorced but I still have my mom. I mean, even though she put me on restriction and stuff, at least I know that she cares about me.

I turn back to my desk and crack open my Tolstoy novel (with the cover still slightly crumpled but taped back on), and get back to work.

Chapter 26

After like, a week and a half of being grounded (which translates to nine days of me being on my best behavior), Friday morning finally arrived and I was praying for an early release from my mother's sudden and inexplicable totalitarian rule. I was up, dressed, and in the kitchen grabbing a Pop-Tart to take to school when my mom walked in and said, "About this weekend."

"Yeah?" I look up at her all nervous, positive she's going to extend my punishment."

"Would you be all right if I left you here alone?"

Is she kidding? "Sure," I answer as nonchalant as possible. "Why? Are you going somewhere?"

"Your aunt Sandy invited me down to San Diego for the weekend. I'm leaving after work and I won't be home until Sunday."

"Okay," I say, trying to contain my excitement.

She looks at me very seriously. "You've acted very mature this last week, so I'm going to end your restriction now. I hope that I can trust you while I'm gone?"

"Of course you can," I say.

"Good." She looks at me steadily. "Have a good day at school. I'll see you on Sunday." She goes into her bedroom to get dressed for work, and I can barely wait to tell M the good news.

But I don't see her until history class since all the cheerleaders were away on some kind of school spirit field trip. So I just walk in and wave at her on the other side of the room and go to my desk. After roll call, my teacher walks up to the chalkboard and starts writing down all these random dates. And with each new one he shouts, "What happened on this date?"

And then everyone gets all competitive to see who can yell out the answer first. I'm just sitting there, staring at the chalkboard, and none of it looks familiar. I mean, the only date I've memorized is the one on my fake ID.

I try to look interested and involved, and I even flip through my textbook trying to find an answer, but the truth is, I don't even know what chapter we're on. So after awhile I just give up and put my head on my desk and I stay like that until the bell rings and my teacher doesn't say a word about it. He gives us an assignment right before he releases us but I don't waste my time writing it down since I know I won't be doing it anyway.

I wait for M outside the door and we walk toward the student parking lot. "What's going on this weekend?" she asks.

"I don't know. I don't have any plans, but my mom's out of town, and I'm off restriction."

"Really?"

"Yeah, really," I say.

"Wanna go to LA?" She opens her car door and throws her books in the back.

"And do what?" I ask.

"Do whatever," she says, starting her car.

Something about the way she said that makes me suspicious, but I'm tired of being under house arrest. So against my better judgment, I throw my stuff into the back and climb in.

We're in this boutique on Robertson when M goes, "I've got a plan. I'm going to nonstop shop. I'm going to swipe this credit card until it bleeds. And when the bill comes in, and my dad tries to confront me with it, well I'm just gonna inform him that I saw him with a certain redhead at the Hotel Bel Air and ask him just what he plans to do about that."

"Uh, that's called blackmail," I say.

"I don't care."

She's loading up on all kinds of stuff and trying to convince me to do the same. And while I may be tempted, I just don't feel right about being part of that plan.

My job in the fitting room is to make stacks of yes's and no's as she rapidly works through the piles of clothes. She just sort of throws stuff on the floor when she's done with it, kicking the piles with her foot. And it bugs me to watch her do that since I work in retail and I'm the one that has to go in later to clean it up, just like I'm doing now.

She tries on a pair of dark denim jeans and they really rock. "Here, try these on, they'll look good on you," she says as she takes them off and tosses them at me.

So I squeeze them over my hips and zip 'em up. God, they fit perfect, low and tight, these are seriously the coolest, but when I look at the price tag, it's more than I make in two weeks, and there's just no way I can afford it. So I hand them back to M and think about how much it sucks living in Southern California when you're impoverished. It's such a celebrity stuffed, look-at-me place, and if you're gonna live here you've got to try to keep up. I mean, sometimes I wish I didn't care about having stuff, but I just can't help it. I'm a resident.

I help her carry all the bags to her car and then she hands me the one with the cool jeans, and goes, "Here, they look better on you anyway."

I hold the bag in my hand and go, "I can't take these from you."

"But they're not from me. They're from my father. Enjoy."

"But what if he finds out?"

"God, you're such a Girl Scout. Relax, he won't find out. Besides, he does not want to mess with me right now. He just doesn't." She slams the door, and starts the car and pulls into traffic.

So we're driving around, trying to figure out what to do next when we see the Java Daze sign and decide to go in. It's this really cool, independent coffee bar and last time we went there we saw Brad and Jen wearing tank tops and cargo pants and drinking chai teas.

M orders her coffee first and I hate to admit it but she's a totally typical California coffee drinker. You know what I mean? It's like, "I'll have a café latte please, but with skim milk not two percent, and with nonfat whipped cream, and I'll put my own sprinkles on so if you could just give them to me in a little cup on the side please." By the time she's finished it's like the next day already. When it's my turn I just order, "One latte, fat and bitter." My god it's just coffee, you know?

So we're sitting at this table and I'm just playing with the foam on my latte while M is sitting there counting her sprinkles. I know she's looking for just the right number and then she'll add them into her coffee. It has something to do with calories, or numerology, or feng-shui. I forget. I mean, it's just one of her quirks.

I notice these two guys at another table and they're really cute and I can tell they're looking at us, but they're trying to be all cool about it, you know like, Okay maybe I'm looking at you but if you don't look back it's okay because I'm secure and girls like me. That kind of thing.

So I look away and start drinking my coffee because if they want to talk they know where to find us. And then like two minutes later I hear someone go, "Hi, my name's Guy."

And I look up and one of them is standing right next to me with his hand extended, waiting to be shaken.

So I shake his hand and go, "I'm Alex, this is M."

Then M looks over at the other table and goes, "Well, what about your friend over there?"

Guy starts laughing and waves his friend over and we start rearranging the table and chairs so there's room for everyone.

"So, what's your story?" M asks Guy's friend Mark, when we're all settled in.

He just kind of shrugs and goes, "Well, we were just out . . ."

"No, no, not that stuff. I mean like what do you do?"

So Mark looks at Guy then he goes, "Oh, well, we're both in grad school."

"Really?" M asks as though she's truly fascinated. "What are you studying?"

"We're both studying economics. And then I'm going on to law school." He smiles at her.

"Hmm," says M. "Well then maybe you should give me your card, I have a feeling I'm going to need a good lawyer someday." She leans in and smiles and Mark has the look of a grand-prize winner.

"So what's your story?" he asks, leaning in closer to her.

M looks at me briefly then goes, "Well, Alex and I are both finishing up our undergrad and planning a big trip to celebrate."

"A trip?"

"Yeah. We're planning a trip to Europe. We're leaving in three weeks!"

"Where are you guys going?" Guy looks at me. But I have no idea where we're going on this fantasy trip so I just look at M.

"Oh, we're just traveling around. We're doing the whole Eurailpass thing. We'll probably end up in Greece or something. We'll be gone for the whole summer, maybe longer."

"Wow, that sounds great," he says.

I look at Guy smiling at me and I feel really bad about lying, but now that it's out there I have to play along. So I smile back and nod my head and say, "Doesn't it? Doesn't it sound great? I really can't wait."

We're finishing up our coffees when Guy goes, "Hey, I know it's short notice and all but there's a party tonight in Brentwood, if you guys want to go. Or if you're busy now, I can just give you the address and stuff and maybe we can meet up later. There's supposed to be a band, so it should go on pretty late."

I kind of want to go, I mean, I think it could be fun, and he's really cute. But then M goes, "Oh, that sounds great, but we already have plans. Maybe some other time?"

So we exchange numbers and say good-bye and when we're back inside the car I go, "What are these other plans we supposedly have?"

M looks at me and says, "Don't tell me you wanted to go to that stupid party in Brentwood?"

"How do you know it was stupid?" I ask.

"Oh, please. It's probably some retard frat party with a bunch of drunken college boys trying to get to third base."

"I thought they were nice, and really cute too," I say, defending them.

"Yeah? I thought they were dweebs. I've got something much better lined up for you anyway."

"What?" I ask, staring at her.

But she just looks at me and smiles.

Shit. I knew she was up to something back in the school parking lot when she was trying to act all spontaneous about coming up here. I mean, let's face it, M's always got a plan. And now, like it or not, I'm part of it.

Chapter 27

I'm just looking out the window, listening to some CD, and not talking to M since I've now asked her three times where we're going and she just keeps saying, "You'll see."

And when we pull into the driveway, I can't say I'm surprised but I'm definitely pissed. "Why are we here?" I ask.

She just looks at me and goes, "He invited us."

"Why? I thought you guys broke up?"

"We made up." She shrugs.

"What? When?" I ask.

"The other night, on the phone. And don't be so judgmental. I really like him."

"But what about the panties and stuff?"

She rolls her eyes and pulls the key from the ignition. "There is no 'and stuff,' it was just those stupid panties, and he explained it to me and it made sense. I was clearly overreacting."

"Are you kidding me?" I look at her like she's crazy. "What could he have possibly said that could make you think you were overreacting?"

M gives me an impatient look and says, "They have maids, and a lot of house guests. This is his parents' house you know."

"So?"

"So, the maid makes the bed. It's not like Trevor does that. She washes the sheets too, so the underwear got tangled in the sheets in the wash and ended up in the bed like that. That's why I didn't find them until the next morning, they came loose in the night."

She looks at me and smiles and I can't believe that she's willing to believe a story like that. I shake my head and look at the house I refuse to go inside of.

She opens the car door and gets out, then stops and stares at me 'cause I'm still just sitting there. "Are you coming?" she asks.

I turn and look at her standing there all excited to see Trevor and totally annoyed with me, and I'm not at all happy about this. I mean, what if Connor's here? So I just look at her and shake my head and say, "No, I'm not coming! And I can't believe you're doing this to me. I mean, what if Connor's inside?"

"Connor is inside." She looks right at me.

"What? Oh my god! How could you do this to me?"

I watch her lean on the door and say, "He knows we're coming. He wants to see you. And I know you want to see him. And you know you want to see him."

"He wants to see me?" I ask, looking at her suspiciously.

"Yes."

"How do you know?"

M just shrugs. "Trevor told me."

"If he wants to see me so bad, why hasn't he called?"

M looks totally annoyed when she says, "I don't know, but now's your chance to ask him."

I stare at her for a minute then look in the rearview mirror and check my makeup. "You should have warned me," I tell her.

"You wouldn't have come if I told you. Come on," she motions with her hand. "It's gonna be great. Trust me."

Then she turns and walks toward the house and after watching her for a moment I get out of the car and follow.

Trevor opens the door and hugs M and looks at me and goes, "Connor ran out to the store. He'll be back soon."

And now I feel like a total loser because I know he ran out because he doesn't want to see me. I bet he was totally suckered into this too.

Trevor goes into the kitchen to get us something to drink and M and I go into that huge room with the pool table and I plop myself onto that same old velvet beanbag chair while M sorts through Trevor's CDs, making piles of which ones suck and which ones rock.

"Are his parents here?" I whisper.

"No. And why are you whispering?" she asks, waving an Oasis CD in the air, not sure which pile to put it in.

"I was whispering because I wasn't sure if they were here."

"Oh, well they're not," she says placing it in the suck pile. "They're like my parent's, totally absentee."

"Maybe you have the same parents," I say. "Do you realize you guys kind of look alike?"

" 'Cause we're both blonde?" She rolls her eyes at me. "Get real."

Trevor walks into the room carrying a six-pack of beer and M puts on some vintage Hendrix CD that she's decided does not suck. There's still no sign of Connor, and I'm beginning to feel anxious and totally annoyed with M, so I get up, grab a beer, and go for a walk down the hall.

As I'm leaving the room I hear Trevor say, "What's her problem?"

And instead of sticking up for me, M just goes, "Who knows?"

I go outside and lay on a lounge chair by the pool. It's quiet and peaceful, and I close my eyes and remember the dream I had last night. I dreamed that I dove into a pool without checking the depth, and my body was sleek, and fast, and careening through the water. All around me it was clear, but right in my path, right in front of me, it was all murky and I couldn't see. I knew I could smash into the bottom at any second and that the only way to save myself was to start climbing for the surface, but I was reluctant to do that because part of me wanted to see the really deep parts. Part of me was curious to see just how bad the crash would be. When I woke up I had this feeling that soon nothing would be the same.

So then someone who smells like soap and fresh air, walks up, casting a shadow over me and blocking what little remains of the sun. "Alex, wake up," he says. And I open my eyes to find Connor standing over me, and my stomach goes all weird, because he's still as gorgeous as ever. "Where's M and Trevor?" he asks.

I look into his eyes, but only for a second, because looking into his eyes can be dangerous, and make me feel things I don't want to. "In that room with the pool table, listening to Hendrix," I tell him.

"I looked in there, I didn't see them."

I shrug. "Then I don't know. Maybe they went upstairs?"

"Mind if I join you?" He sits on the lounge chair next to mine and looks out at the sunset. "Nice colors," he says, motioning toward the sky.

I look at the streaks of pink and orange and purple, colors I wouldn't normally put together, and think how weird it is that even though I slept with him I feel really nervous now. I guess talking is always the hard part.

He turns toward me and says, "I feel bad about the other morning."

I just shrug, but I don't look at him. I focus on the horizon.

"I remembered later that you left your car at Harry's. How'd you get there? Cab?"

I shake my head. "I took the bus." I look right at him.

"You're kidding?" he says, looking surprised.

"I'm not kidding," I tell him. "But it wasn't that bad."

"I'm sorry."

"Are you?" I search his face, trying to find out if it's true.

"Yeah, really." He runs his hand through his hair and he looks pretty uncomfortable.

"You could have told me that at the sushi restaurant," I say.

"I know." He shrugs.

I hold his gaze for a moment, then shake my head. "You know what? Forget it, okay? It really doesn't matter anymore." I look out at the sunset again, and try to get a grip on myself.

"So what have you been doing?" he asks after awhile.

I take a deep breath and decide to be honest for a change. "Nothing, just school and work," I say.

"Where do you work?"

"At a department store. I've worked there for almost two years now."

"Do you like it?" he asks.

I shrug. "It's okay for now. You know, for being a minor and all." I look over at him and he gives me a worried look, but I just laugh.

"When do you graduate?" he asks.

"Soon. A few weeks." I look at him and smile.

"What are you going to do next?"

I look out at the sinking sun and think how funny it is we're having this kind of conversation after all that's happened. "Honestly?" I say, "I really don't know."

"Aren't you going to college?" he asks.

"I messed up. I don't think it's gonna happen for me."

"You could go to, what do you call it? Community college?"

I shake my head and look at him. "God, you sound like my counselor, Mrs. Gross."

"A wise woman." He smiles.

"She wears polyester pants and sensible shoes."

"A fashion-challenged wise woman."

"Maybe." I sit up and put my arms around my knees.

"What do you want to do tonight?" He looks at me.

"I don't know." I shrug, and look away.

"Do you want to get out of here?"

"And go where?" I ask cautiously.

"I don't know, dinner, a club, a movie, somewhere."

"But what about M and Trevor?"

"I've got a feeling they might not surface for awhile," he says.

"Yeah, you're probably right." I roll my eyes. God, I can't believe M. And then I look at Connor and say, "I have to tell you, I was tricked into coming here. And now I'm kind of stuck and have no way to get home."

"I'll take you home if you want," he says, giving me a concerned look.

I shake my head. "It's pretty far. Besides, I'm a pro at the whole bus thing now."

"You're not riding the bus again."

Connor leans toward me and reaches for my hand. I'm not sure I want this to happen, but I fold my fingers around his anyway, because even though I spent a week and a half trying to get over him, it doesn't mean that I did.

His face is close to mine when he says, "I'm glad you're here. I knew you were coming, but I didn't know you were tricked into it. I get the feeling you don't want to hang out with me."

He squeezes my hand and I can feel my entire nervous system running amok. But then I remember how he made me feel disposable and I can't just undo that, so I look him right in the eyes and force myself to say, "Well, I'm not sure that I do."

He looks surprised and shakes his head and goes, "Well at least you're honest."

And I go, "Yeah, for a change." But it's not the truth. It's a big fat lie. Because the real truth is that I want to be with him more than anything.

We go inside the house and while Connor gets a beer, I go searching for the bathroom, only I don't know where the downstairs ones are and this house is so big it's confusing. So I go upstairs to one that I used before.

I stand in front of the mirror and stare at my reflection and wonder what to do. I can't deny the way I feel about Connor, even though I know those feelings are risky. I mean, it took me like, nine days to stop obsessing over him, and now he just appears in front of me and it's like all the bad stuff never happened.

But what if he really is sorry? What if after being without me, he decided that he misses me and really wants me back? I know he didn't exactly say that, but he did say that he knew I was coming over and that he was glad about it.

I reach into my bag, find my lip gloss, and reapply. The best thing to do is just fight the overwhelming urge to jump on top of him and insist on hanging out here at the house in a mellow, platonic way. M and Trevor have got to come up for air eventually and it will be a lot safer for me, emotionally, to not be alone with him. That's it. I'll just hang out and be strong. I look at myself in the mirror one final time, and head out the door.

Halfway down the hall I can hear music coming from one of the rooms, and I'm thinking everyone must be in there. So I push the door open and start to walk in when I see Trevor lying on the couch. He looks up at me and then over at M who doesn't see me because she's busy leaning over a desk, half naked, snorting a line of coke. I just stand there watching her, and I'm totally in shock. When the mirror is clean she looks at Trevor and goes, "Is there any more?" And then she looks over and sees me and goes, "Oh my god, Alex!"

I run down the hall, down the stairs, and into the den where I find Connor sitting on the couch, finishing up his beer. I stand in front of him, short of breath, and go, "Let's go. Let's just go somewhere."

He gives me a concerned look. "Are you okay?"

"Yeah, but let's get out of here."

"Okay." He sets down his beer and stands up. "Where do you want to go?"

"Anywhere."

Chapter 28

We go to a movie and then afterward we grab a pizza and a six-pack of beer and we take it back to Connor's. We're eating it in the living room because there's no table in the dining room, and so we're sitting on the floor, and our knees are touching, and it's really nice and comfortable and platonic.

He puts on some demo CD that he wants me to hear and after two songs he looks at me and asks, "What do you think?"

I cover my mouth because I'm chewing on a piece of pizza and I say, "They're really good. Who are they?"

Then he goes, "Some garage band from Liverpool."

"Oh, you mean like the Beatles?" I ask.

"That would be nice." He takes a sip of his beer and wipes the corner of his mouth with the side of his hand. "You know, I haven't heard anything that fresh and original in a long time."

So I go, "Yeah, they're really good."

"They're brilliant." He nods. "I'm really hoping we can sign them."

He takes another sip of his beer and looks at me in that sexy way that he has and now my stomach is going all weird again and

I'm not sure what to do. I mean, I promised myself I would keep it casual, but it's not so easy when he looks at me like that.

So he moves closer, and puts his arm around me and says, "I'm sorry that things got sort of messed up." Then he kisses me on my hair, right above my ear.

I nod and half smile and say, "Yeah, well, I'm sorry too." And then I look at him and I just have to know, and now's my chance, and I have nothing to lose, so I go, "What about Sam?"

He looks at me intently and goes, "What about her?"

And I go, "Well, are you guys going out?"

"Why would you ask that?" He leans back and looks at me strangely.

And I realize that I can't explain the subtle looks and weird frequency that happens between girls that guys can't tune into, and I guess I never really saw anything concrete anyway, so I just go, "I don't know, I guess I thought . . ."

"We're not dating. She works for me. That's it." He shakes his head and gives me a serious look.

"Okay," I say. But I'm not sure if I believe him.

And then he leans in again and this time he kisses me on the lips. Softly at first and then it grows into something more. And it feels so good, to feel his arms wrapped tight around me, and I find myself pushing into this kiss, pushing into his whole body. And then his hands are on my breasts, and I'm melting into him once again, just like I did the last time. Only this time I know it will be different, because there are no lies between us.

The next morning I wake up alone. I'm still half asleep as I reach over to Connor's side of the bed wanting to snuggle with him, but he's not there and the sheet feels cold, like he hasn't been there for awhile.

I climb out of bed and grab his shirt off the floor, put it on, and holding the front part closed I go looking for him.

I find him in the living room with the phone cradled in his neck putting something into a duffle bag that's sitting on the coffee table.

"Hey," I say standing there.

He turns and smiles and waves and points at the phone and then puts his index finger up in the "just a minute" signal.

So I go into the kitchen and as I'm pouring myself a cup of coffee I freeze when I hear him say, "Okay Sam, six o'clock, don't be late."

He said "Sam." Why would he be talking to Sam? I lean my head toward the doorway trying to hear more, but he already hung up. So I force the whole thing out of my mind because he told me last night that nothing was going on between them. I mean, I'm sure it's just business. And if we're going to be together now, I have to learn to trust him, just like I want him to trust me after all of my lies.

He comes up behind me and says, "Good morning," and then he wraps his arms around me and kisses the back of my neck, and I lean back into him, and he smells so nice and feels so good. And right when I'm thinking how lucky I am that my mom is out of town, and it's only Saturday, and I still have until Sunday night to hang out with him, and how I wouldn't mind crawling back into bed for the rest of the day, he goes, "So why don't you shower, while I make you a big American breakfast, and then I'll drive you home."

Chapter 29

So after a British version of an "American" breakfast consisting of bacon, eggs, toast, fruit, juice, coffee, and a choice of cereals (I mean all the Americans I know just eat Pop-Tarts), we took the long, scenic route home, all the way down the coast to Newport Beach where we stopped for frozen yogurt, and took a walk to the end of the Pier. We talked about things we never talked about before, and I felt so close to him, and so lucky, and I couldn't help thinking how much better my life was now that Connor was definitely back in it.

When he pulls into my high school parking lot, mine is the only car sitting there.

"That's your car I'm assuming," he says as he pulls up next to it.

"Yeah," I say grabbing my purse from the backseat, wondering what to do next.

"I like Karmann Ghias. I think they're really cool."

"It's okay." I shrug.

"So, this is your school?" He cranes his neck around, but all you can really see from the student lot is the tennis courts and the stupid mascot that's painted on the gym.

"This is it," I say, staring at his profile.

And then he leans across and hugs me and I can feel his warm breath in my hair and smell his skin and feel his heart beat under his sweater and it's right next to mine. He holds me like that for a moment then he pulls back and looks at his watch and says, "I should go. Our flight leaves early."

And I go, "What?" And I'm staring at him, trying to make sense of what he just said because I don't remember him mentioning anything about a flight, and the way he just said "our flight" makes me wonder if it's like a surprise for me or something. Like maybe he really is going to take me away somewhere and we can be together and I can just forget about school and all the other things that are dragging me down.

But he looks really uncomfortable when he goes, "I'm going back to London tomorrow."

I sit there stunned, and I feel like I just got the wind knocked out of me, and I don't even know what to say, so I don't say anything.

"Please don't look at me like that. I told you I was leaving," he says.

"You did?" I search his face, trying to remember when he might possibly have said that.

"Yeah. I was supposed to leave a week ago, but it got postponed."

And then I remember. He mentioned something that night at Harry's, but for some reason back then it didn't seem like a big threat, but now it kind of does. And I still want to know what he meant by "our flight" but part of me is afraid to ask because I don't think he meant "our" like "us." But I really have to know so I go, "Who are you going with?"

And he totally avoids looking at me when he says, "Uh, Sam is on my flight."

And I can't believe he said that. And I can't believe that he said it *like that,* like it's just some random coincidence. "You're going to London with Sam?" I ask.

"Yeah, but it's not like you think. She works for me. She's my assistant. She has to come."

He looks at me and smiles and nods, but I just bite down on my lower lip and look away. I mean, I really wish I could believe that story, but I'm not a total idiot.

"Hey," he pulls me back toward him, and touches my cheek softly. "Last night was really great." And then he kisses me, and I let him, but I don't kiss back, and when it's over he says, "I'll write you as soon as I get settled."

And I look at him and go, "You're going to write me?"

"Well, yeah, if that's okay?" He looks confused.

"But why would you write me? I mean, Connor how long are you going for?"

He looks at me closely and goes, "I'm moving back to London. I'll be gone for quite awhile."

"But what about all of your business here?" I ask, even though what I really mean is *what about me?*

He takes a strand of my hair and tucks it behind my ear and goes, "I'm sorry. I thought you knew."

"How could I know?" I'm starting to sound unstable but I don't care. "How could I know if you never told me?"

"But I did tell you I was leaving."

"But not like that! Not like you were moving there! You made it sound like some casual business trip."

"Alex, I'm sorry if you misunderstood, but I'm English, London is home."

I sink down lower in my seat and stare out the window and try to gain control over my emotions because there's no way I'm gonna cry in front of him. "I just wish you were more clear about it. I just wish you had told me before," I say, avoiding his eyes.

"Before what?" he asks.

"Before last night!" I shake my head. God, I never learn, I'm so pathetic.

"Would it have made a difference?"

I look at him and say, "It would have made a big difference, Connor."

He looks at me for a long moment. "I'm sorry," he says.

And he says it quietly, like he really means it. But I just shrug and think how we've said that an awful lot for two people who aren't really boyfriend and girlfriend.

So I grab my purse and reach for the door handle and right when I open it he says, "Alex."

And I look over and he kisses me again and it's nice, but after a moment I break away, and push the door all the way open and say, "Have a safe flight." I resist the urge to finish that by saying *with Sam!* even though it's screaming inside me, wanting to get out.

So I climb out of his car and into mine, and after I start my engine I wave from my window, so he'll know that everything is okay. And when I see him pull out of the parking lot and onto the road, I scream at the top of my lungs for the longest time. And I know I should stop, but I can't. It just keeps coming out. But I don't cry. I won't let myself cry.

Chapter 30

T he next afternoon when my mom returned from visiting my aunt in San Diego I met her out on the driveway and helped her bring her things in. I smiled, and made small talk, and thanked her for the "San Diego!" T-shirt she bought me, even though I don't wear things like that. And I did all this even though I felt like I was in the final stages of death because I promised myself I would keep the whole Connor mess to myself, and just get through it alone.

I go back into my room where I was working on the tenth page of my *Anna K* paper but I decide I need a break. So I pick up the phone and call M just to see what's up, since the last time I saw her she was cracked out on coke. And even though I'm mad at her for tricking me into going to Trevor's and all the other shitty things she's done to me lately, I'm also kind of worried about her.

When she picks up on the fourth ring, I hear her yell, "I got it, Mom! Shit. Hello?"

I go, "M?"

"Hang on," she whispers. And then, "Mom, it's just Tiffany, all right?"

I go, "M, it's Alex."

"I know."

"Well, why did you tell your mom I was Tiffany?"

"Okay. Listen. I didn't know how to tell you this but I guess I have to and I hope you'll understand."

I just listen.

"Remember when my mom found that stash?"

"Yeah, I remember."

"Well, she confronted me and wanted to know what I was doing with it. She was really mad, and I was scared, and so I said it wasn't mine."

"You didn't tell her it was mine did you?"

"Not exactly."

"What the hell does that mean?" I yell.

"Alex, please. Don't be mad. I didn't actually say it was yours. She just sort of assumed."

"Why would she assume that? I've never done drugs!"

"I know, I know. Look I guess she just thought . . ."

"What?" I demand.

"I guess she just thought, well, you know, because your parents are divorced and your mom has to work, and you're not doing that well in school, well I guess that made her think that they were yours."

"All of those things are supposed to make me a drug user?" I scream. "You didn't even stand up for me? I can't fucking believe this!"

"Alex! Listen! I tried to tell her that it wasn't you I was holding them for but she didn't believe me. It's like she convinced herself that I was trying to protect you or something. Anyway, what's the real harm here? It's not like we hang out with my parents. As long as you don't call here or come over when they're home, we can still totally see each other at school and hang out in LA on the weekends. It's really not that big a deal."

"Not that big a deal? Fuck you M."

"But Alex!"

I slam down the phone. And then I pick it up and slam it down again. And then I do that one more time. And when it starts ringing I'm amazed to see that it's not broken. But I don't answer it because I know it's M and I don't want to talk to her.

My mom must have heard me screaming because she comes in my room a few minutes later and when I see her I start sobbing uncontrollably. Then she comes over and hugs me and I feel like I'm six years old again.

"What's wrong?" she asks, her voice full of concern.

"Everything," I say. "I hate my life."

"Don't say that. Tell me what happened."

I wipe my face on the hem of my tank top and go sit on the edge of my bed. My mom comes over and sits next to me and puts her arm around me and waits for me to start. So I tell her all about M and her drug use, and how she told her mom they were mine. And instead of getting mad, instead of saying what I thought she would, my mom goes, "Poor M."

"Poor M!" I practically shout. "What about me?"

She looks right at me and says, "What about you? You and I both know the truth. I know those drugs aren't yours. But look what M's reduced to. Lying about her behavior and blaming you." She shakes her head, "There's something very sad about that girl."

"About M?" I say incredulously.

My mom looks at me and nods, "Yes, I feel sorry for her. She always seems like she needs a hot meal and a hug."

"M? That I've known forever? That M? Like, what could be sad about her? She has *everything* and she always has! She's going to Princeton, she's beautiful, and smart, and popular, and rich."

"Yes, and you're all those things too, minus the lying and the drug use."

I shake my head, "That's just delusional," I say.

"Maybe we're not rich like M's family, but you're beautiful, and smart, and you used to be involved with a lot of different friends, you used to be on the honor roll, you used to be college bound too. Somewhere along the way, you just seemed to give up on all that. But that was a choice you made, it wasn't something that just happened to you."

I sit there with my head in my hands going over what she just said. I mean, I guess I always knew that I was the one blowing it, but I've also been acting like it's not my fault. "I'm such a loser," I say. "And I'm a liar too." I take my hands off my face and look at my mom. "I told a really big lie to someone I cared about, someone I thought I loved, and he dumped me because of it. And then I lied and pretended he didn't dump me, and then I got caught in that too. And then I saw him last night, and part of me hoped all the bad stuff would go away and we'd be together. And everything was so great, and it felt so right, but today he went back to London, and he went with someone else."

"Who is this boy?" she asks.

I shrug. "Just some guy I met. His name is Connor. He's from London. He was here on business."

"On business?" she says, somewhat alarmed. "How old is he?"

"Twenty-three," I say.

"Don't you think that's too old for you?"

I just look at her and go, "I don't even know anymore. I mean, before I didn't think so, but after everything that's happened, I just don't know."

And then I can't help it, I just start crying again, and she hugs me for the longest time and I just cry until I'm empty.

Chapter 31

t's weird at school not hanging out with M at lunch and trying to pretend like I don't see her in class. The first day in French she kept trying to get my attention but by AP History she had totally given up. I guess it's a good thing that we never did sit next to each other.

Tiffany came over to my locker recently and asked what's going on with M and me. I pretended I didn't know what she was talking about.

She said, "For your information, there are two freshmen sitting at the tree that you guys have been eating lunch at since ninth grade. And I never see you guys together anymore."

I knew she was just looking for a juicy story and that really annoyed me so I said, "God, it's not like we were dating you know."

"Well, M said . . ."

I didn't stand there long enough to hear the rest of that. While I have no idea where M is eating lunch, I'm sure she's not answering Tiffany's questions. I mean, she can't be feeling very proud of what she did.

So I'm actually going to all of my classes, getting there early, and paying attention. I have to admit I feel a little lost in most of them; it's kind of like sitting down in the theater just half an hour before the movie ends and trying to figure out what you missed.

About a week after Connor left I got a postcard from him with a picture of the Queen on it, and then a few days later he left a message on my machine. I admit that I listened to the message more than twice, but when I was done, I erased it, even though I had the option to save it for thirty days. And then I sent him a postcard too; it had a picture of Richard Nixon and Elvis; it's called "The President and the King."

Even Guy (remember him, from Java Daze?) called and left a voice mail message, but I'm not sure if I'm gonna call him back. I mean, I thought he was really cute and nice. Not a dweeb like M said. But I lied to him too and pretended I was in college and stuff. Well, technically it was M's lie, but it's not like I tried to stop it. And I'm just not sure I'm willing to start something that's based on lies again.

I went out with Blake the other night after work. Nothing special, we just went to that little coffee place by the store. I didn't plan on telling him, but when he asked, "How's M?" The whole story just came spilling out.

When I was finished, he whistled and said, "Wow, that's ugly."

I go, "Tell me about it."

"Does she know that Connor left?" He breaks his biscotto in half and offers me a piece.

"I have no idea," I say, taking it and swirling the Italian cookie in my cappuccino.

"Well, you know M's always been a little bit of a princess and all, but you guys were best friends."

"Since we were eight," I tell him.

"Listen, you've got to think of a way to work it out. Has she tried to apologize?"

"Several times." I take a bite of my now soggy cookie.

"But you're not accepting apologies right now?" he asks.

"Nope, not right now." I look at him and shake my head. "Look, I'm really mad, and hurt, and offended. She totally lied! She totally betrayed me! I mean, M's mom can think whatever she wants. I don't care about her. But the fact is M didn't even try to stand up for me. She just saw an easy way out and went for it. She threw me overboard and saved herself, and I think that's messed up. Jeez, Blake, if nothing else she could have said they were Tiffany's."

He gives me a horrified look and says, "Don't even say the name. Is she still around?"

"She's still around. Anyway, let's talk about you." I take a sip of my coffee.

"Finally." He smiles.

"When are you leaving?"

"Middle of June."

"I'm gonna miss you." I reach across the table and squeeze his hand.

"Of course you are. But wouldn't you know it, right when I have everything in order, I meet the man of my dreams." He finishes his biscotto and wipes the crumbs from his mouth.

"Are you serious?" I ask.

"Very."

"Blake, you've said that before," I remind him.

"I mean it this time. His name is Ken, and he's gorgeous, and smart, and he cooks." He uses his fingers to list those attributes.

"Wow, I'd settle for just smart. So what are you gonna do?" I ask.

"By June he'll be so in love with me he'll follow me anywhere, right?"

"Totally." I nod my head in agreement and drink the last of my coffee.

"The question is, what are you gonna do?" He looks right at me.

I put my head in my hands.

"How many times do I have to tell you that you can do whatever you want? You're smart and talented. You're setting your own limits you know. You don't need your dad, or Connor, or anybody else. But you've got to get it together." He reaches across the table and says, "High School is almost over, and you're wasting your life if you stay here."

When I got home I was still thinking about what Blake said. The idea of being stuck here for another year after everyone else has moved on is too horrible to imagine. I mean, everyone keeps asking me what I want to do and I realize that I'm no closer to an answer. So I grab a piece of paper and make a list of the five things that I like to do. Kind of a modified version of the aptitude test they made us take sophomore year.

At the top of the list I put READ/WRITE. Which I know sounds totally hypocritical considering my grades and all, but I'm not talking about textbooks and essays. I mean, I really like to read and write fiction, but even though Mr. Sommers liked that one story, I'm not sure if it's like, a realistic goal.

Next I put CLOTHES. But it's not like you can make a living buying clothes for yourself (unless you're M's mom). So that means you have to shop for other people and I kind of already do that right now. So I definitely know that I don't want to do it forever.

Third is MUSIC. But I can't sing or play an instrument so I'm not gonna get too far with that. And I don't know how to run a record company like Connor. And I'm no longer delusional about running a record company *with* Connor.

At number four I put HANGING OUT. But the only people

who can make a career out of that are the Hilton sisters. And I don't think I need to explain at this point how I'm not exactly related.

And number five was blank. Oh well, it's not like it's a *real* aptitude test.

Chapter 32

So after days and days of secretly obsessing about it more than I care to admit, Mr. Sommers finally starts passing out our graded short stories. When he gets to Christine the Collector's seat, I admit, I'm practically standing on top of my desk to get a glimpse of her grade. On the upper-right-hand corner of her paper is a large, red, unmistakable C. Wow, I bet she's never received one of those before. Underneath it is a short note, also in red ink, that unfortunately I'm unable to read from such a distance. She looks at her grade and quickly turns her paper over, and when we make eye contact she looks like she's about to cry. And I gotta tell you, I enjoy every minute of it.

So he hands out all the short stories in his stack and walks to the front of the room. But my desktop is still empty and when I look around I notice that everyone has their paper except me. And now I'm in a total panic thinking that maybe he somehow lost mine. I mean, that would be just my luck, to actually complete an assignment only to have the teacher lose it and assume I didn't do it.

But then he goes, "I'd like to read you a story that I thought was very good."

And then he reads my story, just like last time.

When he's done reading it, someone goes, "Did Alex write that one too?"

And when he answers, "Yes," everyone turns to gawk at me and I know that they're shocked that it wasn't just a fluke the first time.

When Mr. Sommers returns it to me, there's a big red A in the upper-right-hand corner, no note, just a single letter.

Christine the Collector glances at my paper and asks, "Mr. Sommers, is this going to count toward our final grade?"

When he says yes, she drops her head on her desk and sits like that even after he dismisses us. And this may sound crazy, but part of me actually feels a little sorry for her.

When I walk out the door M is standing there waiting for me. But I'm feeling so good about Mr. Sommers reading my story out loud, and giving me an A, that I just can't be mad right now. I look at her briefly and say, "Hey," then head to my locker.

She's right behind me when she says, "Alex, that was a really great story."

So I stop. And I turn, and I look at her and say, "Thanks." Because even though I haven't talked to her in quite a while, the stories I write are really important to me, and it makes me feel good when people say that.

"I never knew you were such a good writer," she says, following me.

And I can't help it. I'm a sucker for a compliment. So I smile and thank her again, and open my locker and switch my books.

"Your characters are like, so real," she says. "It's really amazing how you do that."

I've got my backpack balanced on my knee, trying to get my books inside, when she goes, "Trevor told me that Connor went back to London. I'm really sorry. I'm really sorry about everything that's happened."

I just look at her and go, "Okay, I hear you. I hear your apology, okay?" Because now I know that all those compliments on my story were just a way for her to get my attention so I would forgive her.

"But you won't accept it?"

I shake my head and reach into my locker and grab those jeans she gave me that day we were shopping on Robertson. They still have the tag on them, because I never wore them.

"What's this?" she says, holding up the jeans trying to figure out where they came from.

"You gave them to me that day you tricked me into going to Trevor's. They've never been worn. So you can keep them, or return them. I really don't care."

"But I gave them to you. I don't want them back," she says, holding them down at her side so that one of the legs is dragging on the floor.

"Yeah?" I slam my locker shut. "Well, I don't want them either. You can't buy me stuff then treat me like shit. You can't bribe me into being your friend. I may be poor, but I'm not desperate."

"I wasn't bribing you! I never said you were desperate!"

I just look at her and go, "I don't even know who you are anymore." Then I turn and walk away. I just can't be her friend right now.

When I got home from school I asked my mom if she wanted to rent a movie or something and do you know what she said?

"I'm sorry, but I can't. I have a date."

Wow. I would be big-time lying if I told you that didn't make me feel totally pathetic. I mean, I'm happy for my mom don't get me wrong, but it's pretty weird when she's getting all dressed up for dinner when the most I can hope for is a "very special episode" of *Seventh Heaven*.

So around seven-thirty, her date comes to the door and I answer it because she's still in her room putting on the finishing touches.

He's tall and dressed all business casual, and he goes, "You must be Alex."

I go, "That's me."

And he goes, "I'm Chris."

We shake hands and I invite him in and tell him to have a seat on the couch while I go get my mom. While he's walking toward the living room I totally check him out and I've got to say he's pretty handsome for an old guy in his forties.

So I go down the hall and knock on my mom's door and when she opens it, I go, "Mom, your date's here."

And she asks, "Are these shoes okay?"

And when I look at her I can't believe how pretty she is. I mean, I knew she was pretty but this is different. This is the glamorous kind. I tell her, "Those shoes look great. You look beautiful."

She looks really happy and gives me a quick hug and kiss and when I look in her mirror I can see a faint lipstick mark on my cheek but I just leave it there. "So, Mom, how long have you and Chris been dating?" I ask.

"Are you checking up on me?" She looks at me and smiles.

"Yeah. Unfortunately I have nothing better to do." I sit on her bed and watch her fix her hair.

"We've been dating for about a month I guess."

"Well, he's really handsome. Is he nice?"

"So far." She looks at me through the mirror and shrugs.

"Where did you meet him?" I ask.

"He's actually a friend of your Uncle Terry."

"Do they work together?"

"Yes," she says. Then she asks, "Have you talked to your father lately?"

I lie down on the comforter and look at the ceiling. I can't believe she's going to quiz me about my dad while she's getting ready to go on a date. "No," I say. And I'm thinking I should probably get up and leave now before this goes any further.

"He hasn't tried to call you?" she asks.

I'm sitting on the edge of the bed and I am not about to have this conversation with her, so I go, "No, he hasn't tried to call, because he doesn't give a shit about me, okay? We've already been through this."

My mom just looks at me for a moment with her eyebrows raised and I don't know if it's because I used the *s* word, or because of what I said about him not caring.

"Alex, between your argument with M and your relationship with your father I'm worried about the amount of energy you spend on being angry."

I roll my eyes and go, "What's that supposed to mean?"

She comes over and sits next to me and puts her hand on mine. "I want to share something with you that might help you put things in perspective, and I probably should have told you this a long time ago."

I'm still sitting on the edge of the bed, ready to bolt at any minute because she looks like she's going to say something really serious and the truth is I just don't know if I'm up for it. But she still has her hand on mine and she's looking at me all intense so I don't bolt, I just sit there.

"When I was growing up," she begins, "my father, your grandfather, was an alcoholic and a bum. And I was angry. Angry at my father for not being able to control his sickness, angry with him for constantly embarrassing our family. But I was also angry at my mother, for putting up with him, for being dependent on him, for not protecting us from him."

She gets this faraway look in her eyes and then she bites down on her lower lip just like I always do. And I sit there stunned because I never knew that about Grandpa, but then she never really talked about him before now.

"And when he died, I felt guilty. Guilty because I had secretly wished for it every night that he came home late, smelling of alcohol and starting fights." She shakes her head and looks at me. "And my mother, your grandmother, who never seemed happy when he was around, completely fell apart without him. And so I became responsible for raising your aunt Sandy and taking care of the family. And I was angry again. Because that was her job. I was supposed to be a kid, out running around having fun, not stuck at home making dinner for my helpless mother and my baby sister."

She gets up from the bed and walks over to the mirror where she rechecks her makeup and runs her index finger gently under each eye. "I swore that as soon as I could I was getting out of that house no matter what. Then I met your father, and we married, and we were both far too young." She turns and looks at me. "He came from a similar background, and we just sort of glommed on to each other. Well I know that we both had bad examples of marriage and problem solving, but still, when your father left I found myself very angry all over again. I was angry at being saddled with kids to raise on my own. I was angry with him for walking out on his responsibilities. And I was angry at the way I had let my life turn out."

She comes over and sits down next to me again. "I know I haven't been there for you much, and I worry about the bad example we've given you, because I see you making similar mistakes and I don't want you to repeat my patterns. I want so much more for you." She reaches up and touches me briefly on the cheek. "I know your father abandoned you, and M betrayed you, and I know how much that hurt. But you cannot control other people's actions. You can only control your response to them. And you have to pick your battles wisely, because it just takes so much energy to be angry. Energy that you can put to better use. Your father has limitations that have nothing to do with you. And I'm sure that someday he will have a lot of regrets. But it's time you held yourself accountable for what happens next. And not to use your past as an excuse for not getting where you want to go."

She looks at me for a long time and I just nod. It's a lot to process.

Then she pats me on the leg and asks, "Do you think Chris fell asleep out there waiting for me?" She gets up and grabs her purse and when she opens the door she looks back at me and goes, "What are you going to do tonight?"

I look at her and smile. "Believe it or not, schoolwork."

I sit on her bed until well after I hear them leave, and I think about everything she just told me. I guess I never saw my parents like that before. As real people still struggling to cope with their pasts and the shit their parents dealt them, just like I'm trying to deal with their bad decisions.

And I guess my mom is right. I've spent a lot of time and energy being angry with my dad and blaming him for everything bad in my life. And even though I can't help but hope that he'll have some big-time regrets someday, that's really between him and his conscience.

I'm glad my mom's dating again but it feels kind of weird to witness. I wonder if this means she's finished being angry with my dad?

Chapter 33

T he next Friday after school I'm walking to the parking lot when I run into my guidance counselor. I had successfully avoided her since that last meeting, but it looked like my luck had just run out.

"Alex, how are you?" she asks, approaching me.

Shit. I can't just keep walking and ignore her so I go, "Um, okay. You?"

"Fine. Do you have a minute?"

Damn! I look at her and jangle my keys and say, "Well, I was really on my way home. I mean, the bell just rang and all."

"This will only take a minute." I just stand there hesitating and then she goes, "Don't you have a minute to talk about your future?"

I should have run. But instead I just follow her into her office, like a big retard, and sit in that same old chair in front of her desk and look around. Everything is just like last time, except the plant is missing. I bet she killed it.

She sits at her desk, folds her hands together, and leans toward me. I'm trying not to squirm but she's already making me really nervous. "You haven't held up to your end of the deal," she says.

"What deal?" I fidget with my silver hoop earring. I have no idea what she's talking about.

"The deal where you got your grades together. Early reports on your semester grades are very troubling." She looks right at me.

I look over at the filing cabinet. "Don't you want to pull my file?" I ask. "You know, just to make sure?"

"I don't need to see your file to know that you're failing."

I look at her hair that's permed poodle tight, but just for a second, and then I focus on her outfit. She's wearing a light blue crisply ironed cotton blouse, a belt with flowers painted on it, and pleated white cotton twill pants. And I'd bet you anything she's wearing high-rise, full coverage, cotton crotch, underwear.

"I thought after our meeting you had a firm understanding of what you needed to do to get into a decent school. But you've let your grades suffer to the point where the best we can hope for is community college, and that's only if you graduate."

There's that "we" again. They act like this is a team effort or something. "So, what's so bad about community college?" I ask.

"Nothing, provided you're motivated enough to even go there." She looks frustrated and reaches her hands toward me, palms up. "You are a very bright girl, and it's such a tragedy to watch you waste your potential like this. You are capable of so much more. But I'm afraid if you don't apply yourself this very minute, and if you don't do extremely well on your finals, you will not be graduating with your class. Your future is in jeopardy Alex."

She's looking straight at me and she's trying to get to me, trying to reach me, but I can't stand it so I sink lower in my chair and stare at the floor. We just sit there quiet like that for the longest time. I mean, I don't owe this woman anything. And I don't remember making a deal with her. She railroaded me into all of this and she wouldn't listen when I told her I couldn't do it anymore. If I want to mess it all up, well, that's my business. She can just go back home to her photogenic family and forget this ever happened.

We just continue to sit like that and I can feel her staring at me and I don't know what to do, so finally, I reach into my backpack and pull out the paper I'd been carrying around all week. It's my latest short story, the one with the big red A on it. I look at it for a moment and then hand it to her and go, "I'm trying, okay? I really am. I'm going to all of my classes, and everything." And then I start crying. What a total dork.

She doesn't come around the desk and try to hug me, thank god. She just reaches across her desk, grabs a tissue, and quietly hands it to me. After awhile she says, "I didn't know you liked to write."

I twist the tissue around and around and go, "It's just something I do sometimes. I'm not all that serious about it."

"Why not?"

I just look at her, "What do you mean?"

"Well, you enjoy doing it so much you even do it in your free time. Your English teacher seemed to be impressed and from reading the first paragraph I am too."

"I've got others," I say.

"Okay, now we're getting somewhere." She sets my story on her desk and looks at me. "You don't have to love History and Economics, but you have to get through them to get to the good stuff, the stuff you do like. I know your grades in French are okay and English too, but it's not enough. You can't graduate on that alone."

"But even if I do start applying myself, or whatever, I still won't get into a good school for next year. I mean, I've totally blown it, and my dad told me he won't pay for it anyway," I tell her.

She looks at me steadily and says, "You're young, and very bright. You can still go to a good school and get a scholarship. Maybe not next fall, but there's still the year after that. But you can't just put it off until then. You have to start trying now. You have to graduate."

I look at her for a moment, and it's clear that she really does care. She's not just trying to shame me. Then I look at the picture on her desk of her kids and husband and I wonder if she means well with them too.

"There's a statewide, library-sponsored, teen fiction writers contest." She stops and shuffles around inside her desk until she finds the papers she's looking for. Then she picks one up and reads from the back. "The winner will receive a two thousand dollar scholarship, and the chance to compete in the nationwide finals for additional scholarship money, a trip to New York, and publication in *Sixteen* magazine." She sets it down and looks at me. "I'd like to enter your story, if it's not too late. What do you think?"

"No." I shake my head emphatically.

She gives me a disappointed look and it makes me feel bad, but I'm not budging. "Why not?" she asks.

"I don't compete anymore," I tell her.

"Competition is healthy."

"Only for the winners," I tell her. "Not for the losers."

"It inspires people to do better, to be better."

"I'm sorry. I can't," I say, avoiding the look in her eyes.

She sits there for a moment and then without saying anything she gets up from her desk and leaves the office. But I'm not sure if she's done trying to convince me yet, or if I should stay seated for round two. So I just sit there for a while staring at the floor, and then I grow a little bored, so I pick up one of those papers about the contest and start reading it. But then I hear her coming back and I don't want her to see me reading that, so I fold it up and stick it in my bag real quick.

"I'm sorry," she says, rushing back into the room. "I have to pick up my daughter from school now. But I do hope you'll take me seriously about your grades, and I do hope you'll reconsider this contest."

I just nod as though I'm already considering all of that, and then I grab my backpack and head for the parking lot.

When I get home I grab a container of strawberry yogurt and a spoon and sit in front of the TV and try to find something interesting to watch. But as I flip through the channels I keep thinking about what Mrs. Gross said about graduating, and how close I am to not doing it. And the thought of having to go to summer school, or even worse, returning to that dreadful place next year is unbearable. So I turn off the TV and go into my room, determined to open my textbooks and get my act together.

I change into some sweats and sit at my desk, and just to boost my confidence, I prop my latest short story with the A on it against a stack of books so I can steal a glance at it every now and then when I start to get a little bored (which is inevitable since I'm going to devote one hour to each subject that I'm failing, and that's pretty much all of them).

When I'm well into economics, my second study subject, my phone starts ringing. I stop reading and stare at it, and I hate to admit it but that might be the first time it's done that since Connor left and I stopped hanging out with M.

I watch it ring until it goes into voice mail and then I go back to my book and focus on reading because I promised myself I would get through this without distractions.

But not five minutes later my purse starts ringing so I close my book and walk across the room to get it. I mean, just because I'm not going to answer it doesn't mean I can't look at the display and see who's calling. But I get there too late and now it just says "missed call."

So I turn my cell phone off and start to toss it back into my purse when I see that paper I took from Mrs. Gross's office all crumpled up inside. I smooth it out against the hard wood of my desk and read through it quickly, and I'm surprised at how simple it is. I mean, it's basically an application that just needs to be filled out, attached to a story, and then mailed in. I don't know why but for some reason I thought it would be more complicated. I thought it would be a bigger deal.

So I grab a pen and start filling in the boxes in all capital letters. (I'm not sure why I use all caps. I guess I just think it looks more official). And then I sign my full name at the bottom with a little more care than usual.

But that was the easy part. Because when I pick up my story and read through it, I start to feel panicked at the idea of some professional editors reading it and judging it. I mean, I know it's a contest with judges, but I mean *judging it* like, "that story sucks," kind of judging it.

I can't do this. There's just no way. I throw the application on the floor and stare at it lying there on my ugly, outdated, shag carpet, and I wonder when I got so used to losing. Just two years ago losing didn't even occur to me, but now, it's like I expect it.

But I don't want to be like this anymore and maybe the only way out is to start trying again. I mean, maybe if I send it in secretly, without telling anyone, then I'm the only one who will know if I fail. And it won't be that big of a deal since I'm used to it anyway.

I pick up the application, prop it up next to my story, and stare at the big, red A on the title page for a long time.

If I don't try I won't lose, but then I won't win either.

Chapter 34

So on the night of the prom, do you know what I'm doing? I'm going on a date with Guy. I guess I started feeling a little sad and lonely, and I had no other prospects. My mom was going out with Chris again, Blake was nervously meeting Ken's parents, and I heard Tiffany announce in a very loud voice in the girls bathroom that M was going to the dance with her mother's tennis buddy's son. Can you believe it? I mean, there was just no way I was gonna sit at home by myself. So I decided to return Guy's call.

He seemed pretty happy that I called him back and as we were talking I decided to come clean. I just couldn't stand the idea of another lie out there. So when he asked me about the weekend I mentioned that it was prom but I wasn't going. That way he could be the one to sort of drag it out of me.

So of course he goes, "What? The prom? I thought you were in college?"

So I take a deep breath and I go, "I know."

He sounds confused when he says, "What?"

"Well I guess I just didn't want to admit that I'm still in high school. It's like, you guys are in grad school and stuff, and well, it just seems so juvenile." God, I sound like a dork.

So then he does the strangest thing. He starts cracking up. So I just sit there, holding the phone, not really knowing what to do, when he goes, "Well, I guess if you're gonna come clean then I'll come clean too, we're not really grad students, we're freshmen at UCLA."

I totally can't believe this, but I talk myself out of being upset, because that would be hypocritical. So I go, "Why did you lie?"

And he goes, "I guess for the same reason you did."

"Wow."

"Does that mean there's no trip to Europe either?" he asks.

"Only in my dreams," I tell him.

So then he goes, "Hey, if you don't have a prom date, I'd be honored to take you."

I swear that's just how he says it, kind of old-fashioned but I like it.

"You know what, Guy," I tell him, "I have no interest in the prom. Why don't we just go to dinner or something instead?"

"Done. I'll pick you up Saturday at seven."

So Guy knocks on my door at seven sharp and when I peek at him through the peephole I see a very cute, kind of preppy, Paul Ruddish–looking guy, which was pretty much how I remembered him.

When I open the door he goes, "Wow, you look great."

I'm just wearing my favorite low-cut, boot-cut jeans, a white baby-T, a little black blazer I bought in the boys' department at work (I like the way it's kind of shrunken looking), my favorite black, super-high-heeled Steve Madden, platform sandals (which kill to walk in but I love them), and my hair is wavy, loose, and long.

I smile and say thanks and start to close the door behind me when he goes, "Are your parents home?" Like he's all prepared to make a good impression on them or something.

I just laugh and say, "No, my parents haven't been in the same house since I was twelve. They're divorced. My mom's on a date."

"Isn't that the weirdest?" he says as he opens the car door for me. "My parents are split too, and it's so bizarre when they start dating about the same time you do."

He gets into the driver's seat of his very cool, black Jeep Wrangler and starts the engine.

"I like your jeep," I say as he pulls out of my driveway.

He looks at me and smiles. "It's not the most comfortable ride, but I like to mountain bike and hike and stuff so it comes in handy."

I nod and smile and say, "The closest I've been to the great outdoors would be the boardwalk in Venice Beach."

"No, that can't be true?" He looks at me briefly and I nod my head that it is indeed true.

"Well, we'll have to change that. I know some great spots for hiking and horseback riding, right here in Orange County. I grew up here."

"You did?" I'm not sure why, but I'm surprised to hear that.

"Yeah. Well not here, but in Laguna Beach."

"Oh," I say. "Well that may be part of Orange County, but it's way cooler than here."

"True." He looks at me and laughs.

"Did you have a horse?" I ask.

"Yeah, I still do. I have two. I keep them at my mom's house."

"I used to have a horse," I tell him as I look out the window. "A long time ago."

When we get to the restaurant he goes, "I hope you like Indian food."

Now normally, in the past, I would just lie and say I love it, and try to fake my way through it. But I'm not lying anymore, unless I absolutely have to. So I say, "Well, I've never had it before."

He smiles and says, "Then you're at the right place because the food here is great, so if you don't like this, then you'll know you don't like Indian food."

He helps me translate the menu into food groups I'm familiar with, then we just order a bunch of different plates so we can share. And I have to say that even though some of it is surprisingly spicy, I think it's absolutely awesome.

We enjoy a really nice dinner together. I mean there are a few awkward moments of silence, but for the most part he keeps it going pretty well and he's interesting and easy to talk to. And I've only compared him to Connor a few times and even then I've tried to stop myself because that's just not fair, it's like apples and Oreos really.

So after he pays the check he goes, "Hey, let's do something fun, something different. Are you up for it?"

"I'm always up for fun and different," I say.

"Good, then let's go bowling!"

"What?" There's just no way I heard him right.

"Yeah, bowling." He's laughing and looking at me expectantly. "They have this late-night thing called 'rock 'n' bowl' and it's really fun. They turn the lights down low and they use these black lights that make the pins glow fluorescent. And the music is great. C'mon, Alex. What? Do you think you're gonna lose?"

"Yes, of course I'll lose. I haven't bowled since grade school," I tell him.

"That's why it will be fun. Listen we can do the whole bar, club thing if you want, but that scene gets so old after awhile."

And hearing him say that, I've got to agree. Suddenly I don't feel like hanging out in some smoky scene, drinking and trying to act like I belong. I don't know if bowling is the answer but it's worth a try. "Do you know where there's a bowling alley around here?" I ask.

"As a matter of fact I do."

So we go bowling. I take off my cute sandals and replace them with some ugly red-and-green flats, and some socks Guy purchased from a vending machine. Then I grab some weird, shiny, bright pink ball I can barely lift, stick three fingers in it, and give up all hope of looking cool while I hurl it toward the fluorescent pins. I mean, if you're going to bowl well, you have to be willing to look like a dork.

I start off good, getting a few strikes and spares, but my game quickly falls apart and turns into a series of gutter balls. But it doesn't really matter 'cause it's not like we're playing competitively or really keeping score, which is good for me since Guy just happens to be a great bowler.

We are having so much fun that we want to keep playing but they're getting ready to close up, so Guy looks at me and says, "So, what's next?"

I look at my watch and I'm amazed to see that it's almost one o'clock. It's not like I have a curfew but I've been having so much fun, I'm sad to know that it's almost over.

"Um, I don't know," I say. "It's kind of late."

"You want to get a coffee?" he asks.

And even though I'm glad to see that he's reluctant to end it too, I shake my head and go, "We're in Orange County, remember? Everything closes early. But I have coffee at my house if you want."

"Should we head there?"

I look at him and smile and nod, and I hope that he doesn't think I'm trying to seduce him by inviting him back to my place.

Chapter 35

When Guy pulls into my driveway I'm praying that my mom and her date won't be here because it would be way too weird to hang out on the couch, making small talk with them. But all the lights are off, and I don't see Chris's car anywhere, so I'm hoping that means the coast is clear.

We walk in the door and Guy is right behind me with his hand on the small of my back and I'm getting kind of nervous and I'm wondering if this is still about coffee. I mean, he's totally cute, and really nice, but I'm just not ready to fling myself on the couch and start making out with him, so I go straight to Mr. Coffee and start filling up the glass carafe and locating two clean mugs that don't have anything embarrassing printed on them.

"Nice house!" Guy shouts, competing with the sound of grinding beans.

"It's okay." I look at him and smile and shrug.

"Is this you?" he asks, picking up a silver frame that holds a picture of a naked, bald, fat, drooling, eight-month-old, which unfortunately is me.

"Uh, yeah." I cringe. "Hey, why don't you go put on a CD in the living room?" I say, hoping he won't see the picture of me in my Girl Scout uniform that my mom insists on displaying.

I put two mugs full of coffee, a little porcelain cow filled with cream, and a couple cubes of natural sugar on a tray and carry it into the living room where Guy is hanging on the couch humming along to that Jonny Lang CD I bought right after Connor dumped me the first time.

"Oh, you like Jonny Lang?" I ask, trying to hide my dismay as I set the tray on the table.

"Yeah, he's awesome. I saw him perform a couple years ago, he was amazing."

I smile at him and add some cream to my coffee, stirring it slowly and watching the colors blend then change, and I'm wondering how I can ask him to choose a different CD without seeming weird. It's like, I feel really nervous being alone on the couch with him because I know he's probably going to try to kiss me soon and I think I want him to, but I wonder if it will be creepy if he does it with that CD playing in the background. I know it sounds kind of stupid, because I'm sure that plenty of people own it, but I think of that as my own personal soundtrack for when I lost my virginity.

So we're just sitting next to each other, drinking our coffees, when Guy sets his down, looks at me, and goes, "I'm glad I met you. I had a lot of fun tonight."

"Me too," I say, and I'm wondering if he's getting ready to leave or something, because that's the kind of thing you usually say right before "good-bye." But then he leans in and kisses me and it's so unbelievably good, that I suddenly couldn't care less who is singing in the background because now it's all about Guy and me and nobody else exists.

His arms are around me and his hand is buried in my hair and I'm clutching the fabric of his shirt, pulling him closer, and kissing him deeper, when I hear someone say, "Uh, you left the door unlocked."

We spring apart. Practically to opposite sides of the couch, and I'm wiping my mouth, and shifting my top around, and I'm not even looking up because I have no idea how I'm going to explain this to my mom, but then I hear Guy go, "M?"

And I look up and see her standing right in front of me, wearing her prom dress. "What the hell?" I say, and it comes out sounding really angry because I am really angry, but I'm not sure if I should be angry in front of Guy.

"Sorry," she shrugs. "Am I interrupting?"

"Uh, yeah," I say rolling my eyes and trying to tone down the anger, even though the sarcasm is loud and clear. "What, you don't knock?"

"I did knock, but you didn't answer so I tried the door and it was open." She sits down on the lumpy ottoman, and runs her hands over the front of her dress and I can't believe she's actually making herself comfortable, because there's no way I'm letting her stay.

"I should go," Guy says, looking at M and then me.

"No," I say. "Don't go. M won't be long." I give her a menacing look, but she doesn't notice because she's busy rummaging through her tiny prom purse.

"M, what are you doing here? Why aren't you at the prom?" I ask, sliding back toward Guy, and reaching for his hand.

"Prom sucked," she says, setting down her purse and reaching for a sugar cube that she plops into her mouth. "Fucking Tiffany won Prom Queen." She shakes her head.

"Of course she did. What, did you wanna win it?" I ask incredulously.

"No, I didn't. It's just, this night is just totally annoying. And I miss you. I just wanted to go out and do something fun like we used to. Come on, what more can I say? I'm so incredibly sorry, I mean it. And I really need to talk to you."

"What happened to your date?" I ask, glancing briefly at Guy. I really don't want him to know about our argument.

"My date? I went to the prom with Harry Potter. I'm not kidding. He was four feet tall, wore thick glasses, and I think he was ten years old. I made a total fool of myself and then I sent him home. I thanked him, and told him he could keep the boutonniere, and I sent him on his way."

Guy laughs out loud, but all I can think is that's karma for you.

Then she looks at Guy and goes, "Hey, Guy, I'm sorry for crashing your date."

He just shrugs and squeezes my hand.

"Is there any coffee left?" she asks.

I glare at her and I can't believe she refuses to get the hint and pack it up. But I just go, "Yeah, I'll get you some. You look like you could use some coffee."

"Thanks," she says. And I can't tell whether she means it or whether she's being sarcastic, but I don't really care either.

When I walk back into the living room I hand M a cup of coffee in an unfortunate mug that has, That's my girl! printed over a picture of a little kid in an orange baseball hat. But it's a picture of my sister this time, not me. She takes a sip of the coffee and looks at Guy and goes, "So what's your friend doing tonight?" She sits up straighter and smiles hopefully, like we're gonna fix her up on a date at one-thirty in the morning.

"Mark? I don't know, I think he's on a date."

"Figures," she says, slumping down again. "Story of my life."

She nods her head and picks at the tacky corsage she's still wearing and I wonder what she could possibly mean by that. From my vantage point it always seems like guys jump through hoops for her.

"Hey, M, there's something I've been wondering?" Guy asks, taking a sip of his coffee.

"Yeah?" she looks at him warily.

"Well, you don't have to tell me if you don't want, but, what's your real name?"

She looks at me and we both start laughing.

"I'll tell ya but it's gonna cost," she says.

"How much," he asks, reaching for his wallet.

"How much is it worth to you?"

"Ten bucks?"

"Never!" She shakes her head and gives him an offended look.

"Twenty?"

She narrows her eyes at him and goes, "Okay, but no checks, no credit cards, just cash."

Guy tosses a twenty on the coffee table and M swiftly picks it up and stuffs it in the top of her prom dress.

I sit next to Guy and wait for her to say it. She heaves a big dramatic sigh and says, "Madison. My name is Madison."

Guy gives her a disappointed look. "I want my money back! I thought it was going to be something awful, like Matilda, or something. Why do you go by M?"

She looks at me and I answer for her, "Because since her first day of kindergarten all the way until junior high, at least one article of her clothing was always monogrammed. I mean, sometimes it was her T-shirt, or sweater, or even her socks, but there was always at least one big blue M. After awhile people just started calling her that and it stuck."

Guy looks at her and shakes his head, "I would have never pictured you as the preppy, monogrammed type."

"That was back when my mom still picked out my clothes," she says.

So we're drinking our coffees and it's kind of weird because I really want M to leave so I can hang out with Guy and kiss him some more, but she just keeps sitting there in no apparent hurry to be anywhere else and it's really pissing me off but I don't want to have it out with her in front of him so I'm acting all normal like this is fun, but it's not.

So finally Guy looks at his watch and goes, "I gotta go."

And I look over at M but she just sits there, and I know I won't be able to get rid of her without a lot of drama, so I just surrender to the situation and look at Guy and go, "Okay. I'll walk you out."

We're standing next to his Jeep when he says, "Is your friend gonna be alright? She seems upset."

And I think it's weird that he said that because if anyone is upset it's me. But I just say, "Sorry about all that."

Then he leans in and kisses me and it's really nice and completely amazing and when he pulls away he goes, "Next time, let's go horseback riding."

And I smile and say, "Okay."

When I go back in the house M has abandoned the ottoman for the couch. And she's sprawled out on it, and her shoes are off and her feet are propped on the coffee table. So I go over to the CD player and turn off Jonny Lang since it's now my soundtrack for making out with Guy, and I put on a Tori Amos CD because it doesn't remind me of anyone. And then I look back at M and I'm so pissed at her for just showing up like that, and barging in, and I'm just about to tell her, but something about the way she looks, lying there like that, makes me go, "Are you okay?"

She sighs heavily and scrunches her face into the palms of her hands like she's trying not to cry. She sits like that for awhile then she says, "Shit, Alex, I'm so sorry. I've been such an ass."

I sit on the ottoman and face her, but I don't say anything because I totally agree.

She wipes her face with the hem of her prom dress and looks at me and goes, "Trevor and I broke up."

I just sit there and stare at her, and I know I'm supposed to say something, but to be honest, that really doesn't make such a big impact anymore. I mean, not after the last time.

"What happened?" I ask.

"Prom sucked. The whole night was a disaster. So I left early and I kept trying to call Trevor on his cell but he wouldn't answer. So I drove all the way up to LA, and long story short, I caught him with another girl."

"I'm sorry," I tell her.

"It's my own fault," she says, shaking her head. "I should have dumped him the last time. I can't believe the lies I let him feed me, just so I could keep hanging out in that whole, stupid, shallow scene." She shakes her head and looks at me.

"He kept trying to act like I'm just as bad, you know. Like it's my fault he was out with another girl, since I was out with another guy at the prom. And I'm like, 'Trevor, you didn't want to go to the prom, remember? You told me to go and have fun.'" I watch her reach over and pick a tiny rose off her corsage and hold it up to her nose.

"He knows damn well that the only reason I went to the prom is because it's supposed to be some kind of big deal, and that for the last few months, I haven't dated anyone else. And because of that, I didn't have anyone to go with, so as everyone knows I was set up on a date with a fucking Hogwarts reject. I had a terrible time, the whole night sucked! All I wanted was to find Trevor and be with him. It never even occurred to me that he was totally taking advantage of the situation. Asshole!" She shakes her head and throws the rose across the room, watching it land on a hanging plant.

"M, did you find out who she is?" I ask.

"Oh yeah, that's the really brilliant part. It's his fucking ex-girlfriend that he's told me all about. Can you believe that? So I go, 'Hey Trevor, the definition of ex means prior not current. It means past not present. It means then not now.' Then I told him that he's a fucking loser for jumping back into a pool that he already peed in. Then I told him to *fuck off!*"

She covers her face with her hands and she sits like that for awhile. And in the background I hear Tori Amos sing, "Never was a cornflake girl, thought that was a good solution."

After awhile she sits up and looks at me and goes, "I know you think I'm totally spoiled and that my life is one long easy ride. And maybe in some ways, it's true. But that doesn't mean my life is perfect. Far from it." She reaches into her purse and pulls out a tissue and presses it against her nose for a minute.

"You know, sometimes I feel like I've been dumped in the middle of the ocean without a life vest, but everyone just expects me to be able to swim to shore, and break the speed record, and get a gold medal for doing it. It's like, everyone has these huge expectations of who I should be, you know, 'M's a cheerleader, M gets good grades, M's going to Princeton. Mommy and Daddy's perfect little M.'"

She shakes her head and rolls the tissue up into a tiny ball. "I'm so fucking perfect that they don't even have to pay attention to me. I'm so fucking perfect that they wouldn't even consider that those drugs were mine. Do you know how much that hurt? That my mom was so unconcerned about me that she just pawned the whole thing off on you? And do you know why she did that? Because that made it easier for her."

She looks at me for a moment, then she puts her head in her hands and starts sobbing these giant, shoulder-shaking tears. I just sit there and watch her cry, and think about what she just said, and I can't believe how alike we really are. It's like, we've both been really busy sabotaging ourselves. Just messing up anyway we could, hoping someone would pay attention. But the people we want to notice just don't care as much as we wish they would and there's nothing we can do about it.

She wipes her face on the hem of her dress and says, "I'm sorry about messing up your date, really."

I just look at her and shrug. "Don't worry about it. We're going on another one."

Chapter 36

*G*raduation is just two weeks away and I'm definitely earn-
ing my diploma. It's like, on the nights I'm not at work
I've stuck to my new routine of turning off my phone, TV,
and stereo (anything that might distract me), and spending an hour on each of my subjects. It's kind of like being on restriction again, only this time it's self-imposed.

When I finished my *Anna Karenina* essay I actually held on to
it for two full days before turning it in. I just didn't know how to
go about it. I mean, I didn't want to walk up to Mr. Sommers's
desk and give it to him in front of the whole class, and I really
didn't want to stay late and give it to him when no one was there.
So one day when he got called out of class for a few minutes and
everybody started acting all wild, I went up to his desk and slid it
under some other papers and hoped that he'd find it, but not until
after the bell rang.

And even though I feel like I'm making some progress, it still
seems like I'm the only person in this whole damn school that
doesn't have the slightest clue of what I'm going to do this summer. Practically everyone is either going on some great vacation,
or on a major nonstop shopping spree for their new college
wardrobe, and of course M is doing both. Her family is cruising

the Greek Isles, and then stopping in Paris for a few days on the way home so she can load up on cool stuff to wear at Princeton. I'll probably just put in more time at the store and wait for something to happen.

I talked to Guy a few times, but I've only seen him once since that night with M 'cause we've both been pretty busy studying for finals.

So I'm just sitting in my room, taking a break from my French workbook, and reading my numerology in the new *Elle,* when the phone rings. I'm assuming it's M so I pick it up on the first ring.

Someone with a British accent goes, "Alex!"

And I go, "Connor?"

And the connection is kind of strange so I know he's still in England. And he says, "What's up?"

And I want to pretend that tons of things are up, you know. But the truth is this magazine I'm reading has pretty much been the zenith of my day. So as part of my new honesty campaign I say, "Nothing."

So then he goes, "How's school?"

And I say, "Great!" Which isn't as big of a lie as it would normally be. "How's the band, did you sign them?"

"We did, and I think it's going to be really big. I'll send you some studio tracks later. Hey, I heard Trevor and M broke up," he says.

"Yeah." I close the magazine and put my feet up on my desk.

"Wow, that's too bad."

"I guess."

"So when are you coming to London?" he asks.

"What?" I say. I mean, is he joking?

He laughs and goes, "When are you going to visit me?"

So of course I give a nervous laugh, and go, "Um, I don't know."

"Well, think about it. It could be fun."

So then we chat for maybe a minute more and hang up. And I sit at my desk wondering what that was all about. It wasn't long ago that I dreamed about going to London with Connor. I thought that would solve all my problems, and change my life. But now,

I'm not so sure. And like, what would happen once I got there? Would I be his girlfriend? And more important, do I even want to be his girlfriend?

I guess after all that happened it never occurred to me that I would ever go there. But then I never really thought I would hear from Connor again and this is the second time he's called.

But maybe I could go there. I mean, I have nothing else planned, and I've even managed to save a little money from working at the store.

So on my way to work I stop at a bookstore and pick up a travel guide to England. You know, just to skim through it and see what it's really like there.

About an hour before closing Blake calls me from the Men's Department.

"Alex," he whispers, "I just gave Ronette my two weeks' notice."

"No way," I say. "How'd she take it? What'd she say?"

"She wished me luck and great success. She was so nice about it I didn't get to say anything nasty to her. And then she hugged me."

"Gross."

"Yeah, it was kind of. What are you doing?" he asks. "Because it's dead over here."

"It's dead here too," I tell him. "I've had two customers all night. But I don't care 'cause I got this book on London and it's pretty much taking up all of my time." I close the book and run my hand over the picture of Big Ben on the cover.

"Don't you think you're maybe taking your Richard Branson fantasy a little too far?" he says.

I just laugh and say, "No, it's not about that. Connor called and he invited me to visit."

"Are you going?" he asks cautiously.

"I don't know." I twist the phone cord around my wrist and turn to look at myself in the mirror.

"Did I tell you that Ken's moving to New York with me?"

"Are you serious?"

"Yeah, his company has an office there. He's putting in for a transfer and there's a really good chance he'll get it. You know it would be really great if you came to New York this summer too. Between me and your sister, you've got plenty of places to stay."

"You don't think I should visit London?" I ask him.

"It's not London I don't think you should visit."

"Oh, you mean Connor."

"Well, I'm just worried about you."

"What do you mean?"

"I don't want you to get hurt," he says.

"Well, what about giving someone a second chance?" I ask.

"Alex, the only one you should be giving a second chance is you."

Chapter 37

After work I go to M's house. Her parents are out for the night at some charity dinner, and we're just taking our time getting ready to go out. And I feel kind of guilty because I'm sort of halfhearted about being here. I mean I'd really rather be home studying for next week's finals, because our friendship just isn't what it used to be, and I'm kind of over the whole going-out scene. But she kept going on and on about how it was our last big night out before summer and college and all that stuff, and I figured that one more night out on the town wasn't gonna kill me. But just to be safe, I made her promise that no matter what, we wouldn't end up at a club. I know it sounds crazy to be jaded at seventeen and a half, but I just can't help it.

So M's painting her toenails in a color called Tangerine Dream with her right hand and drinking a glass of her parents' champagne with the other. While I'm rifling through her closet looking for something cool to wear.

I'm only halfway through one of the dress racks when I go, "Are you really gonna take all this stuff to college with you? I mean, you're gonna fill up the entire dorm room just with your clothes."

M looks at her overflowing closet and shrugs. "After my mom's done pilfering, you can have whatever I don't take."

"Really?" I ask.

"Yeah, why not?"

I pull out a suede halter-top I've coveted all year, and slip it over my head. Then I pull on some suede pants I found folded on a shelf. I walk over to the full-length mirror and gaze at my reflection. Then I turn to M and go, "Pocahontas?"

She looks at me and laughs. "Totally."

So I take it all off and start over.

Then M goes, "Did I tell you that my dad cornered me about the 'extravagant,' as he puts it, balance on the credit card?"

"Oh my god, no. What happened?" I grab a black silk skirt off a hanger.

"Nothing happened. I just explained that if he wanted to really experience an *'extravagant balance'* he could just wait and see what the divorce was gonna cost him when I tell my mom about his mistress."

"No way!"

"Way."

"But I thought your mom already knows and isn't doing anything about it."

"Yeah, she knows. But he doesn't know that I know that she knows. He was so floored by me knowing that he just sat there all red in the face and then he started yelling at me about some totally unrelated situation. So I stood up and told him that as much as I enjoyed our little chat, I had other places to be."

"What'd he do?"

"Nothing. Bastard." She rolls her eyes. "Hey, have you talked to your dad since that big argument?"

"No." I just look at her and shrug.

M nods and goes, "God, I hope when the time comes we can pick 'em a little better than our moms did." Then she pours more champagne into her glass, takes a sip and goes, "What are you gonna do?"

"What do you mean?" I ask. "After graduation? I have no idea. Why? What are you gonna do?" I pull a lacy, silk camisole over my head and search her shoe racks for something I can walk in.

"Apparently I'm going Greek Island hopping and then on to Princeton."

I reach down for a pair of kitten-heeled sandals and sit on the edge of the bed while I slide them onto my feet. "What do you mean 'apparently'?"

M takes a sip of her champagne and goes, "I don't know. Sometimes, it just doesn't feel like it's my decision. Sometimes, I just wish I could cut my hair short, dye it blue, and say 'fuck you' to my mom and dad. You know, in a note, on the fridge. It's not like they're ever around so I could say it to their face." She looks at me and laughs.

"That's just nerves," I tell her and reach for one of her little denim jackets.

"What if it's not?" she says, and she really looks panicked.

"You're gonna be fine. I promise."

She goes over to the mirror and runs her fingers through her long blond hair, and gazes at her perfect reflection. "Yeah, you're right." And then she turns and looks at me and goes, "Do you realize you haven't mentioned Richard Branson lately?"

I look at her and roll my eyes. "Yeah, I guess I'm getting a life, huh?"

I'm searching in my bag for some lip gloss when she goes, "Heads up!" Then she tosses a robin's-egg-blue box at me.

"What the——?" I catch it before it hits the floor and stare at it in my hand.

"Just open it," she says.

So I pull off the white ribbon, and remove the top, and inside I find this really cool, silver, Tiffany charm bracelet just like the one she wears that I've always admired. She even had my initials engraved on it. I hold it up in front of me and ask, "What's this for? I mean, it's not my birthday or anything."

"I don't know. I guess it's for graduation." She shrugs.

"But I don't have anything for you!" I say.

"Okay, then it's not for graduation. Listen, I guess it's just sort of a thank-you present for being such a good friend." She takes a sip of her champagne and looks at me. "I mean it, even after what I did to you, you were still there for me. I totally crashed your date with Guy but you still helped me that night and I don't know what I would have done if you hadn't been there. I was in worse shape than you realized."

I hold the bracelet in my hand and I feel weird about accepting it because sometimes M's gifts turn into bribes. But then I glance at her and she looks so happy and excited and it makes me feel guilty for thinking that. I mean, we've been friends forever and if she says it's a thank-you gift, then it's a thank-you gift. And I shouldn't be so suspicious. And it's not like I don't deserve it. So I put it on, and I admire the way it hangs on my wrist, next to my watch.

So we end up at a club. When we pull into the valet I look right at her and say, "I can't believe you!"

"What?" she asks innocently.

"We agreed. *No clubs*, remember?"

She hands the valet her keys and says, "Relax, it's not a club. It's a bar."

"It has valet parking, a big line, and a cover charge, M. It's a *club*."

"Sorry, Alex, you're wrong. It's called, Bar None. See," she says, pointing to the neon sign over the door. "It's a *bar*."

And I stand there in front of the door and then I look down at the shiny, silver bracelet on my wrist, and I know that, once again, I've been bribed.

Chapter 38

She just happens to know the bouncer from her Trevor days so we don't have to stand in line and we go right upstairs to the VIP room.

I'm not really into the VIP scene like M is. It just seems so pretentious to me. I mean, it's really not so different from the downstairs room except that everyone up here is busy patting themselves on the back for being hip enough to be up here. I really can't stand that self-congratulatory stuff.

So we're sitting in this tiny booth and M is flirting big time with some guy in the corner who just sent over two glasses of champagne from the big bottle that's sitting on his table. And I'm just looking around the room at all these fakers and posers who are acting like this is so important. At the beginning of the year I would have been thinking I was so cool to be sitting here too, but now I just feel tired.

I look over at M and watch her reach into her purse and pull out a joint and a silver lighter.

I just sit there looking at her, thinking there's no way she's gonna smoke that here, in a public place, where it's against the law to even smoke cigarettes.

When she starts to light it up, I get all panicky and go, "M, you're not gonna smoke that are you?"

She gives me this annoyed look and says, "Would you just chill out? I just want to relax a little. You know, maybe you need to relax a little too. It's like, you're so judgmental and you've never even tried it."

I look around the club to see if anyone is watching. A few people are looking at us, but no one seems to care. I watch M inhale and hold it, then go into a major coughing fit as she exhales. And her face is all red, and she certainly doesn't look any more relaxed to me, but what do I know? I mean, maybe she's right. I am kind of judgmental about doing drugs, especially for someone who's never tried any. So I look at her, and go, "Do you think I should try it?"

She looks at me all surprised and says, "Yeah, have at it."

So I take the tiny smoldering blunt from between her fingers and hold it up to my mouth. And I can't believe I'm gonna do this because I made a promise to myself that I wouldn't do things like this. I know it sounds lame, and it's just pot, which is natural, and the Indians did it and stuff, and it's really no big deal, but a while back I made this list of things I wouldn't do and dorky as it seems smoking pot was number three.

But maybe I outgrew that stupid list. Because to be honest I wrote it back in like, ninth grade when I was all into getting straight A's, and being the class president, and all those other activities that I've since abandoned. I mean, I'm just not any of those things anymore, so maybe this is what I am now, a person that smokes pot in the VIP room of a trendy new club.

So I hold it up to my mouth and just as I'm about to inhale I look at M and she's got this huge smile on her face, and she's all excited, and it really bugs me that my doing something that goes against my personal value system would bring her so much joy. So I take the joint and drop it into my champagne glass and watch it float briefly with the bubbles and then submerge."

"What the fuck, Alex?" she yells.

"I changed my mind," I say.

"Yeah? Well you didn't have to drown it! Shit! You wrecked the champagne *and* the pot!" She rolls her eyes and looks at the ceiling. "You're so fucking holy. God, I was just trying to relax a little. Everything is such a big fucking deal with you."

She's glaring at me and I just can't stand it anymore. I can't stand this stupid club, and I can't stand her. But I don't say anything, I just give her a nasty look, grab my purse, and leave.

I go into the bathroom.

There's a crowd of girls at the mirror, putting on lipstick and saying mean things about some girls they know that aren't in the restroom. So I push into an empty stall, grab my cell phone, and check my messages. There are two. The first one is from Connor. He's talking the usual telephone talk, you know "How are you? Blah blah blah." Then he asks me if I've decided about London, because he's reserved a first-class ticket for me on Virgin! I stop and play the message again so I can hear him tell me that a second time, then I push two to save. Then I listen to my next message. It's my dad. So right as I have my index finger poised over three to erase, he tells me he got married last weekend. I feel sick. I don't hit three. I press one to listen to it again and it's for real. It's weird how he doesn't mention who he married. But I have to assume it was Cheri.

Oh my god. Am I supposed to be happy for him? Because I feel totally nauseous. It's the same sick feeling I had that day when I vomited in the bathroom at school. I lean against the door and try to piece it all together.

Let's see, Connor gave me a first-class invitation to London, and my dad gave me a stepmom that's younger than my sister, and named after a fruit. I wrap my arms tightly around myself and try to keep from crying. And I don't even know why I'm so upset. Because the truth is, I was replaced long ago. And I've wasted a lot of time trying to pretend otherwise.

I make my way back to the table, hoping I can convince M to go home, but she's no longer sitting there because she is now at the corner table sitting on top of that Big Muscular Blond Guy with the free champagne.

When she sees me she waves and shouts, "Hey Alex, come over and hang out with us."

So I go and sit with M and her new friends because I don't really know what else to do. I just sit there watching her down like, her fifth drink and at one point when her friend gets up to go somewhere she leans over and says, "Jeez, is he like hot, or what?"

I just look at her and shrug.

And she goes, "What's wrong with you?"

But she doesn't say it like she's concerned. She says it like she's annoyed. So I don't tell her about my dad's message, and the decision I have to make about Connor. Instead I just shrug and go, "You wanna go soon?"

Then she rolls her eyes and says, "Would you please just relax. This is our last big night out! Why are you trying to wreck it? We'll probably never get to do this again, since I'm leaving for college and stuff!"

And right when I'm about to tell her that I don't consider this quality time, her friend comes back and she totally ignores me again.

Eventually we all end up at someone's house and I'm sitting on the couch next to some guy. I have no idea where M is, and I don't even know this guy's name. But he's totally getting on my nerves, because it's all too obvious that he's just looking to get laid. And you know what? I'm just not into it. I'm not saying I'll never have sex again, or that I have to fall in love first. I'm just saying that I want to belong to me for awhile, and not share myself with anyone else.

So I get up from the couch and say, "Excuse me."

And what's-his-name goes, "Where are you going?"

So I stand in front of him and say, "Listen, no offense, I just want to be alone right now."

He gives me an odd look and shrugs. He'll get over it.

I wander around the house looking for M, because I'm not having fun and I'm determined to go, but I can't find her anywhere. So I go outside in the backyard and I see her in the Jacuzzi with her new friend, and they look just like a commercial for some sleazy, new, Reality TV show.

They're both naked and totally making out, but I walk up to them anyway because it's nothing I haven't seen before and I'm serious about going home. I clear my throat so they'll know I'm standing there and M breaks away and sees me and goes, "Hey, what's going on?" and she gives me that same annoyed look that she's given me a lot tonight.

But the truth is, I don't care about looks like that from her anymore, so I just say, "I want to go home."

"What? Now? Uh, I'm a little busy here." And she nods her head toward her friend who is rolling his eyes at me.

"I'm serious," I say. "I want to go."

Then she looks right at me and says, "Well, I'm not leaving, so I don't know what to tell you."

I'm standing in front of her and I'm on the verge of tears. But I also know that this is the very last time that she gets to treat me like this.

I shake my head and say, "Okay then, I'll see you later." And I turn to walk away.

"Yeah, right," she says. "Like where are you going?"

I stop and turn to look at her. I look at her until she starts to get uncomfortable. And then I say, "I don't know where I'm going M, but I'm going somewhere."

Chapter 39

The sun is making its slow ascent, lighting up the sky, but not yet burning off the morning chill, so I wrap my arms tightly around my waist and start walking. And I'm hoping I don't get mugged, or kidnapped, or raped because I'm all alone, and I have no idea where I am, where I'm going, or even how I'll get there. I guess I'm starting to feel a little panicked. I mean, now that I've made my point with M by storming out like that, part of me wants to just duck back in, wait it out, and get a ride home in her comfortable, warm, safe BMW.

The parked cars lining the street are coated in a thick, silvery layer of morning dew, and other than the faint bleeping of a distant car alarm the neighborhood is quiet. I turn the corner on to what seems like a busier, less residential street and I immediately regret it when I see these two guys walking right toward me. They're wearing baggy jeans and similar sweatshirts with the hoods pulled up over their heads, but I can't tell if that's because it's cold out, or if it's so I won't be able to identify them when they're done torturing me.

I glance longingly at the other side of the street and wonder if I should cross before they reach me, but I hesitate too long and now they're coming right at me. So I just look straight ahead and start walking faster and right as they pass me they nod and say, "Hey," and I exhale the breath I'd been holding without realizing it, and I wonder if I'm crazy to be wandering around, by myself, somewhere in LA, when it's still kind of dark out.

I cross the street and walk another block, passing storefronts that will remain locked for at least another three hours, and then I turn another corner for no apparent reason and suddenly I know exactly where I am.

So I head over to this little coffee place that's just opening for business and I get in line behind two of those *Pacific Blue* cops. They turn around and really look me over, but there's no law against getting a latte after a long night, so I just totally ignore them. I mean, it's hard to take a cop in bicycle shorts seriously.

I'm just leaning against the wall, waiting for my order when these two women walk in. They're speaking Spanish, and I watch them point at the donuts in the glass case, and listen to the soft sounds of their language. And it's so nice and musical that I wish I could understand and be a part of it. Then one of them starts laughing at something the other one said, and you can hear that high tinny sound bounce off the ugly tiled walls, and the counter covered in fingerprints, and even the old man behind the register looks up and smiles. I mean, it's really a beautiful thing to hear at six in the morning when you've been up all night, and you've lost your best friend.

I grab my large latte and an oversize glazed donut and carry it out to my usual spot on Venice Beach. I've never been here in the morning like this and it's really nice, serene and peaceful, which are not words you would normally use to describe this place.

Most of the homeless and junkies are waking up or going to sleep, and some of the vendors are slowly starting to arrive. And as I tear a piece off my donut, I think about second chances and how I've been giving them to all the wrong people. And how maybe Blake is right, maybe I'm the one that deserves one.

I mean, it's time I face my future and accept the fact that M isn't really such a good friend to me, and hasn't been for awhile now. My dad doesn't care about me, and now that he's remarried, the sick fact is he'll probably give himself a second chance and have a few more kids. So if I was holding onto any smidgen of hope that he'd come around, well, I'd better just let it go right now.

My grades suck, especially in History and Economics, and there's just no getting around the fact that it's completely my fault. I totally blew my junior and senior years. I just buried the whole thing in a big pile of apathy.

And even though I've been doing better about going to class and stuff, it's still too late for a scholarship and it won't get me into a good school. But that doesn't mean I can't fix it. I mean, maybe it's time I write the story of my own happy ending.

I dig around in my purse looking for a pen and a scrap of paper. I've got to make a list. I've got to have a plan. Because I refuse to be running around like this the same time next year. I want to have something of value.

So at the top of the page I write ME in capital letters, then I underline it. Then next to the number one I put SCHOOL. School is very important. Duh. Okay, I may be a little late in figuring that out but better late than never, right? So what if I have to go to community college for awhile. If I work during the day and go at night, maybe it won't be so bad. And if I really buckle down and get serious then I can wipe out the last two pathetic years, get my A.A., and apply for a scholarship for a better school in a year or two.

At number two I put WORK. The truth is I'd like to be a writer. But until that happens, I could probably do more with the job I have now. I can probably switch to full time after graduation and even inquire about that assistant buyer position that I heard is opening up soon.

Next to three, I put FAMILY. Then I write DEAL WITH IT.

Next to four, I put LONDON. But I'm not going. I mean, it was nice of Connor to invite me, and to offer me a first-class ticket, but I've been sidetracked by too many people for too long. I've wasted a lot of time waiting for other people to start my life for me, and I'm just not willing to put my dreams on hold for some guy. Connor is not my future. And I'm not gonna make the same mistakes my mom made.

I guess I got a little ahead of myself when I numbered the page to five because I really can't think of a fifth. It just always seems that every list should include at least five items. But Rome wasn't built in a day, was it? At least I think that's what they said in AP History.

Then at the very bottom of the page I write, CHANGE IS CONSTANT. 'Cause that pretty much sums it all up for me. Then I carefully fold up my list and put it in my purse and I just lean back and watch the people and try to make my coffee last.

And right when I'm thinking I should probably get up and head home, I see him, the Iguana Man. He's dressed in a pair of dirty old cutoffs and the same old Grateful Dead T-shirt with the same old iguana sitting right there on his shoulder, like it's permanently attached or something. I'm just watching him walk aimlessly down the boardwalk when all of a sudden he stops and looks up. We stare at each other for a moment and now he's cutting across the sand, quickly heading toward me. I look around nervously, hoping I'm mistaken, hoping that there's someone else he's fixated on. But I'm the only one sitting here.

I know I should get up and get out of here, but it's like I've grown roots deep into the earth and I'm unable to move. So I just sit and hold my breath, and pray that he won't recognize me, that he won't speak to me.

As he approaches I can hear the song he always hums under his breath, and smell his strange odor, and my body tenses up in a primal preparation for fight or flight. But when he's right, exactly in front of me, I start to relax. Because the truth is, he no longer scares me. I've got a plan now, a direction, and there's just no way I'm gonna end up like that.

He passes by, as though we'd never met, and goes straight for a big, metal trash can and starts rummaging through it. I watch him retrieve an old, empty beer bottle, and as he's walking away I realize there's something I want to do.

I grab my purse and go after him and when I'm right behind him I say, "Hey, Iguana Man! Stop! I have something for you."

He stops and turns and looks at me and his eyes are still red like last time but I can tell they don't recognize me. I remove the Tiffany bracelet that M gave me and I hold it out to him in offering and say, "Here. This is for you. I want you to have it."

He holds it up and squints at it, then peers at me closely. "Why?" he asks.

I just shrug and say, "I helped someone once and she gave it to me. You helped me, so I want to give it to you."

He looks at me for a moment as though he's trying to place me, and then he just nods his head and puts it in his pocket. And as I watch him wander away I wonder if it ever occurs to him to try another beach, another city, another zip code. Or if he got tired long ago and just gave up. I vow to just keep moving forward, no matter what, because there's just no way it stops here for me.

When I can no longer see him I tell myself I'm ready to move on. And this time I really mean it.

Chapter 40

The last days of school are total chaos, but somehow I manage to keep up with it all. I took the week off work, doubled up on my study time, and even offered to do some last-ditch extra credit for History and Economics. I guess I forgot how much work it is to be a good student, but if they give me a diploma, then it will all be worth it.

I haven't seen much of M. She's missed some days of school and I guess her mom is keeping a pretty tight rein on her now. A few days after I left her in LA, she knocked on my door and apologized while her mom waited outside in the car. She told me that she spent the entire weekend getting high with those guys and when she finally made it home she was pretty messed up. But she just walked right into the kitchen where her parents were having breakfast, stood next to the table until they looked up from their newspapers, then she said, "I have something to tell you."

She told them all about the drugs, and the drinking, and how it had nothing to do with me, that it was all her. I guess her dad started yelling at her but her mom told him to shut up. Then her mom came around the table and put her arm around her daughter for the first time in years and walked her down the hall to her bedroom where they could talk in private.

M's mom made her see a psychiatrist, but after one or two sessions the doctor insisted that her parents go too, and that's when M finally confronted her dad about his mistress. So now her parents have their own weekly sessions, and the trip to Greece and France has been delayed indefinitely, but M seems pretty okay with it. She said it's kind of a pain having them all involved in her life again, and that she can't wait to get out of Orange County, go to Princeton, and get a fresh start in a new place. I have no doubt that she'll totally excel there too.

My sister called on Tuesday and said, "Hey Alex, I bought a ticket to visit you and Mom. And while I'm there I was hoping I'd get to see you in a cap and gown?"

I started laughing. "I think it's gonna happen. I've been studying really hard."

"Congratulations!" she said. "I'm really proud of you."

"So I guess you heard about Dad?" I asked, twisting the phone cord around my arm.

"Yeah, Cheri sent me an announcement. He didn't even call. Can you believe it?"

"Yeah, I can believe it," I said.

"Does Mom know yet?"

"Well," I said. "I was really nervous about telling her, you know? But it didn't go too badly. She just shrugged and said, 'Better her than me.'"

By Thursday, I'd taken all of my finals and although there's no doubt that I could have done better, I didn't choke near as much as I could have. And the good news is they're going to let me graduate.

M waited for me after AP History and asked me if I'd sign her yearbook. She seemed nervous about asking, and even though we're not best friends anymore it still made me feel bad. So she gave me hers and I gave her mine and we took them home over night so that we could write something really meaningful.

But when I got home, I sat in my room and stared at the empty page she reserved for me and I tried to come up with something good, but my mind just kind of went blank. It's like, I've known her forever, and we've had some crazy good times and more recently, some crazy bad times, but I didn't feel like re-capping them, and I've never been very good at the mushy stuff, and I definitely wasn't writing "don't ever change," because change is what it's all about. So I borrowed a line from a Sheryl Crow song and wrote, "Regret reminds you you're alive." Because I guess we've both had a few things to regret lately. And then I borrowed a line from some famous French lady and wrote, *"Non, je ne regrette rien."* Because you just can't regret the things you learned from.

The last day of school I'm sitting at my desk in French listening to the morning announcements drone on and on, stuff about a final bake sale at noon, and last-minute grad night info. And then this, "Congratulations goes out to graduating senior Alexandra Sky for winning first place in the statewide Teen Fiction Writers Contest. Alexandra will be receiving a two-thousand-dollar scholarship award, and will go on to compete in the Nationals for a trip to New York City, an additional five-thousand-dollar scholarship, and publication in *Sixteen* magazine."

I sit at my desk stunned at hearing my name over the loud-speaker. After I secretly submitted my story that day, I just put it out of my mind. I mean, I was so convinced I didn't stand a chance that I didn't mention it to anyone.

Everyone in my French class just stares at me, but then M starts clapping and whistling and they all join in. And I just sit there and smile because *I got a scholarship!* and I never thought that would happen.

When Mr. Sommers sees me at my locker he comes over and says, "Alex, it's been a pleasure knowing you the last few years."

I'm shocked that he'd say that and I look at him and go, "It has?"

He laughs and says, "I'm aware of your attendance record and I'm flattered that you managed to make it to my class more than any other." I just look at him and then he goes, "And congratulations on the Fiction contest. I think you're very talented."

I go, "Really?"

And he goes, "Really. And thanks for the Tolstoy essay."

He smiles at me then and wishes me the best of luck in my future. Six months ago I never could have imagined that happening.

M's parents have invited us to dinner after the ceremony. I guess they're trying to make amends or something. But even though I'm not angry about the whole drug mess anymore, I'm not going. I'm not going to grad night either. Instead I made plans to have dinner with my mom and my sister, and afterward I'm meeting up with Guy for a late-night horseback ride.

My dad never did call or send a card, but I'm okay with that, really I am. I guess he's just busy honeymooning with his virgin bride. Okay, maybe that was a little sarcastic, indicating that I'm not entirely over it, but you know what? I will be. I'm working on it. After all it's number three on my list.

And speaking of my list, I carry it around all the time. Even sitting in the hot sun with this graduation gown sticking to the dress that Blake designed and made for me. In one pocket I'm carrying my list, and in the other is the scholarship check that Mrs. Gross presented to me after school.

It was the first time in the last two years that I was called into her office for something positive. When she handed me the check she came around her desk and hugged me and said, "I knew you could do it."

You probably think it's foolish to carry the check around in my pocket. Like, I may end up losing it or something. But no way is that gonna happen. I've finally got a good firm grip on the future.

I look out into the stands and search the crowd and see my mom and my sister. I wave at them and they see me and wave back. And then I see M's parents, the size two and the doctor, but they don't see me, they're too busy looking at all the other parents. Then I look over at M and she rolls her eyes at me and I stick out my tongue at her, and we both crack up.

From FAKE IDs to CATCHING WAVES in the OC. Fresh, funny fiction from Alyson Noël.

"Alyson Noël truly captures what it's like to be a teenager struggling to find herself."
—*Portrait* magazine

"Noël...writes with a bit more humor and authenticity than some of her chick-lit contemporaries."—*Booklist*

Available wherever books are sold
www.stmartins.com • www.alysonnoel.com

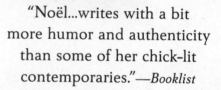

St. Martin's Griffin

Don't miss a single
alyson noël novel

Cruel Summer
Kiss & Blog
Laguna Cove
Art Geeks and Prom Queens

Available wherever books are sold
www.alysonnoel.com

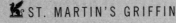
ST. MARTIN'S GRIFFIN

Enter the world of
the immortals

"Addictive. I couldn't put it down. I dreamt about this book.
And when I was finished, I couldn't get it out of my head.
Simply breathtaking." —*Teens Read Too* on *Evermore*

For free downloads, hidden surprises,
and glimpses into the future

Visit www.ImmortalsSeries.com.

Can't get enough of The Immortals ?
Then check out the new series all about Ever's little sister, Riley!

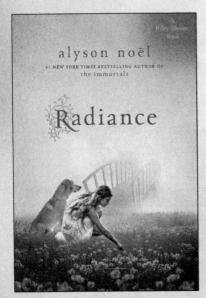

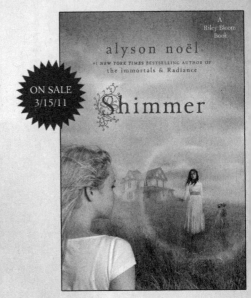

ON SALE
3/15/11

Riley has crossed the bridge into the afterlife—a place called Here, where time is always Now. She has picked up life where she left off when she was alive—but she soon learns that the afterlife isn't just an eternity of leisure. . . .

The *Radiance* story continues as Riley takes us back in time to a place where she is the only one who can set things right.

For free downloads, hidden surprises, and glimpses into the future visit www.ImmortalsSeries.com.

SQUARE
FISH